HOW I CAME WEST,

AND WHY

I STAYED

HOW I CAME WEST,
AND WHY
I STAYED

◆

STORIES BY
ALISON BAKER

CHRONICLE BOOKS

SAN FRANCISCO

For Hans

The stories in this collection have appeared in somewhat different form in the following magazines:

"How I Came West, and Why I Stayed" and "Better Be Ready 'Bout Half Past Eight" in *The Atlantic Monthly;* "How I Came West, and Why I Stayed" also appeared in *Best of the West 5,* edited by James Thomas and Denise Thomas; "Clearwater and Latissimus" in *Ontario Review* and in *New Stories from the South: The Best of 1992,* edited by Shannon Ravenel; "The Spread of Peace" in *Gettysburg Review;* "The Kidnappee" in *The Black Warrior Review;* "Field Notes" in *Willow Springs;* "The Heaven of Animals" in *Alaska Quarterly Review;* "Flatus Vocis" in *The Kenyon Review;* "Missionaries" in *ACM (Another Chicago Magazine);* "Love In the Winter" in *Quarterly West;* "Doolittle's Utopia" in *Ascent;* "Margaret Mead" in *The Laurel Review.*

Printed in the United States of America

Library of Congress Cataloging in Publication Data

Baker, Alison, 1953-
    How I came west, and why I stayed : stories / by Alison Baker.
        p. cm.
    ISBN 0-8118-0324-4 (pbk.)
    I. Title.
    PS3552.A399H68   1993
    813'.54—dc20   92-28963
                                                                      CIP

Cover design: Sharon Smith
Text design and composition: Ann Flanagan Typography
Illustration: Mercedes McDonald
Border design: Zahid Sardar

Distributed in Canada by Raincoast Books,
112 East Third Avenue, Vancouver, B.C. V5T 1C8

10   9   8   7   6   5   4   3   2   1

Chronicle Books
275 Fifth Street
San Francisco, CA 94103

Contents

How I Came West, and Why I Stayed

◆

IT WAS A long, strange trip, over frozen plains and rivers and into the mountains; but when the going got really tough, I'd close my eyes, and there they were: Lisa, in camouflage pants, stalking bears; Debbi, in blaze orange, wheezing out female elk calls till huge bull elk stampeded down the hills, ready to perform.

Now I stood outside the Silver Dollar Saloon, the wind whipping around my collar, my hands like two lumps of ice even in my Thinsulate-lined mittens. The sky was cluttered with stars, but I couldn't stand there staring at them all night. I took a deep breath and pushed my way through the swinging doors.

My glasses steamed up, but I could tell everyone was looking at me by the dead silence that dropped over the room. I took off my glasses and wiped them clean on my neckerchief. Then I put them back on. I'd been right; every head in the bar was turned toward me, and the faces were sort of orange, and puffy looking, in the light from the video games.

I cleared my throat. "I'm looking for cheerleaders," I said.

They looked at each other and then back at me. "What's that?" said an old geezer at the bar.

"I said, I'm looking for cheerleaders," I said.

"That's what I thought you said," the old guy said. He guffawed; and suddenly the whole room erupted in laughter, people pounding each other on the back, slapping their thighs, rolling in the sawdust on the floor. I smiled, glad the ice was broken.

I walked over to the bar and sat down beside the old guy. He was called Ol' Pete. "You cain't never find 'em, not in this weather," he said. The snow had stopped, but the night air was bitter cold. The roads up the pass were closed, with drifts over twenty feet high.

"Haw!" Ol' Pete suddenly guffawed again, and the rest of the heads—hoary, bewhiskered, grizzled—turned back in my direction. "On'y a fool!" he said, and the others grinned and nodded, and chanted, "Fool, fool."

"Buy 'em a round," whispered the bartender as she wiped off the bar in front of me.

"A round on me," I said, and an excited hum swept the room. After the third round the hum broke out into singing, and in the middle of "... deer and the antelope play ... " someone sat down beside me.

"Why you want to go up there, anyway?" she said. I turned and looked her in the eye. She was dark, of indeterminate age, and she wore a buffalo-head helmet, complete with gleaming horns. "They wanted you up there, wouldn't they a took you with 'em?"

I nodded. "I can't explain it," I said. "It's just something I have to do."

She nodded, too. "I can understand that," she said. "It's big—bigger than you, maybe. What's your name, stranger?"

"Most folks call me Whitey," I said.

"It won't be easy, Whitey," my companion said. "I can coach you some, but it'll be hard work."

She said her name was Buffalo Gal, and that I could bunk with her. On one wall of her cabin she had a USGS map, all squiggles, with red-headed pins marking the cheerleader near-sightings. I stared at it but could discern no pattern in the scattered red dots.

"They come and go," Buffalo Gal said. "They might as well be Bigfoots."

"Bigfeet," I said.

"Whatever," said Buffalo Gal.

She worked me hard. She never let up, never let me slack off. "Hit 'em again," she'd say, time after time. "Harder, harder." But she was generous in her praise, too. "Go, go, go!" she'd shout as I telemarked through the quakies. I worked harder for Buffalo Gal than I'd ever worked before; there was something about her that made you want to.

And then one evening, as we skiied through a narrow canyon, Buffalo Gal stopped so fast that I crashed into her. "Listen," she said.

"Give me an *A*," the voice came, faint as starlight, distant as the sigh of a bear in her snowbound cave. It was followed by a wailed response from a dozen throats, "*A*." It echoed down the hills and canyons, and up under the trees around us.

"It's them," Buffalo Gal said.

Saturdays we made the long trek down to the Silver Dollar, just to make contact with human beings, and to have a drink.

"Sure, I heard 'em," Ol' Pete said when I asked him. "Hear 'em all the time."

"Have you seen them?" I said.

"Hell," Ol' Pete said.

When he didn't say any more, I had to ask. "How can I find them, Pete?"

"Haw!" he guffawed, and nods and slow grins spread across the other faces in the room. "Where you from, Whitey?"

"Veedersburg, Indiana," I said.

"Well, then, I'll tell you," Ol' Pete said. "Them cheerleaders is like a poem. You don't go lookin' for a poem; it sort of comes to you, iff'n yer in the right place, doin' the right thing." His rheumy eyes got rheumier, dripping a little, as he watched Lu, the bartender, wiping up some spilled milk. "You cain't predict. You can be out there for days, huntin', trackin' 'em across the range, countin' the buttercups, and you won't see hide nor hair. And then one day you just washed yer hair, or yer mebbe smokin' some weed you saved up from yer last trip south, and there she'll be, standin' afore you, smilin' down at you, her hand stretched out, whisperin', 'Score, Pete, score.'"

"Wow!" I said. "That happened to you?"

"Nope," he said.

Buffalo Gal and I skiied home, heading back out of town and up the canyon through the moonlight. I looked around for shooting stars, and my nose twitched at the smells that skidded across the moonscape toward us: a last whiff of tobacco from the Silver Dollar; the sweet, flowery smell of someone's anti-static sheet from a dryer vent; the mucus-freezing smell of cold air rushing off the mountains. It was just the sort of time I might have seen them, if I'd only known.

In the mountains, in Montana, in winter, time loses its substance; it becomes meaningless. Night ran into day like the Ovaltine that Buffy stirred into our milk in the morning. I knew time was passing by the way the moon grew and shrank; I knew a week had gone by when we headed for the Silver Dollar on Saturday night. But that's all I could tell you.

"That's how it is here," was all Buffalo Gal would say.

One day, up in Avery Pass, we came upon a single, dainty footprint, clear as day, left by a size-seven ripple-bottom gym shoe. I flung myself into the snow beside it. "How could she leave just one?" I cried, and when I put my face next to it, I sniffed just the faintest of odors—rubber? antifungal medication?

"You tell me," Buffalo Gal said. With her ice axe she chopped the footprint out of the frozen snow and laid it gently in her helmet. I pulled it along the ground behind me, the horns serving as runners across the snow. We flew down the mountain, down to the lower pass and back to the cabin, and the speed of our passage created a wind that freeze-dried the footprint, sucked the moisture right out of it. It was frozen so solid it would never melt.

We hung the footprint above the front door, hoping it would bring us luck.

I was beginning to understand how important the presence of the cheerleaders was to the local people. They were part of the mountain mythology, feral fauna as significant as the mountain lion, the grizzly, the Rocky Mountain bighorn sheep. And they were not a recent phenomenon; nor were they exotic visitors. The history of cheerleaders in Montana went back for many, many years: as far back as local memory reached.

Ol' Pete had given me a hint of what they meant. What the manatee is to the naturalist in the mangrove swamp, what the race car is to the Hoosier, what the tornado is to the Kansan—that is what the cheerleader is to the Montanan. Cheerleaders are Possibility, they are Chance, they are Fate; they are beauty, and grace, and poetry.

Many had learned the hard way that Ol' Pete was right: you couldn't find a cheerleader. You had to wait, and be ready. Many an expedition, hunters in their red flannel, stocking up their mules or their llamas or their ATVs with two or three weeks' worth of food, had set out determined—come what may!—to find the cheerleaders. They carried guns, too. "Hell," they'd say, if you asked why. Would they shoot a cheerleader? Would they hang a freckled, pink-cheeked face above the fireplace, among the furry heads of grizzlies and mule deer and moose, and the iridescent bodies of stuffed dead pheasants?

The truth was—the truth was that nobody really knew how he or she might react, if he or she actually found them.

And in all the years the cheerleaders had been in those parts, no one *had* found one. There'd been tracks, and signs: bits of pompom here and there, and of course my frozen footprint, and once an old, well-used megaphone, standing on the wide end under a spruce tree.

But many a hunter had returned cold, frostbitten, disappointed. And many a hunter had hung up her gun, and taken up, say, jogging, or tai chi—something that would get her outside, in the woods, on a hilltop—and in solitude, maybe whispering, she'd chant, "S-U-C-C-E-S-S." Just in case, someday, the cheerleaders came to *her.*

"Okay, B. G.," I said one evening, as we stretched like lazy cats before the glowing wood stove, each with her own bowl of popcorn—Buffy liked garlic powder on hers, but I stuck with melted butter. "What gives?"

"Ah," said Buffalo Gal. She smiled, and gazed dreamily at the stove. "Impetuous Youth."

"Youth?" I said. "Buffy, I'm forty-two years old. I'm not exactly Youth."

She shook her head and gave me a look I couldn't interpret. "Whitey, cool your jets. Do you know how long I've been up here?"

"No," I said.

Buffalo Gal leaned over her popcorn bowl and put her face close to mine. "Neither do I," she said.

"But Buffy," I said, "how do I find the cheerleaders?"

"How the hell do I know?" Buffy said. "I've been up here lo, these many moons, and I haven't found them yet."

When Buffalo Gal said that to me—when I realized that, by golly, she never had said she could help me find them—I had to ask. "Why are you up here, Buffalo Gal?" I said.

She smiled. "Whitey," she said, "I used to be a jock. I did

every sport you can imagine—field hockey, tennis, jai alai. Seems like every time I turned around, there they were, supporting me all the way. 'Go, Buffy! Yea, rah, Buffy!'" She shook her head. "Guess I just didn't want to go on through life without 'em. Even if it's not me they're cheering for any more. I just want to hear them, once in a while in the night. Just want to know they're there."

I nodded, and stood up. "I'm off," I said.

"See you around," she said.

That's the way it is in Montana. When the time comes to go, you go, and there are no hard feelings.

I don't know how far I skiied that night, or how long. I was thinking as I went, and that's a dangerous thing to do. Thinking distracts you. You can get lost, thinking of something other than where you're going. You can ski right up the mountain and over the top, and you get going so fast that it's already too late when you realize there's nothing under your feet and you have taken off into pure, crystal-clear Montana air. Every now and then in Montana you see it—a skier, flying across the moon like a deformed Canada goose.

I don't know how far I skiied, but when the trail ended, I was right where I knew I'd be: at the door of the Silver Dollar Saloon. I went inside, and when I'd wiped off my glasses, there was Buffy, nodding at me, and Ol' Pete lifted a finger from his glass in greeting.

I had sat down at a little table and ordered a glass of milk when someone spoke. "What are you up to up there, anyway?" she said, across the crowded room.

I knew who it was: Renée, a lean, grim-faced ranch hand, not much older than I was. She'd ridden the rodeo circuit for a while and then come back to Montana to work Ephraim P. Williston's sheep ranch. Somewhere along the line she'd lost her left hand—caught in a lasso and squeezed right off when she was roping a steer—and most Saturday evenings she sat in the Silver Dollar with a chamois rag, rubbing and polishing her elk-antler hook till it gleamed. She was a tough customer, Renée; even the feral dogs stayed away from her flocks.

The room was so still you could hear the chamois rubbing against her hook. She stared at me, her eyes in the shadow of the red crusher she never took off. Her hand, polishing, never stopped moving.

I swallowed the last of my milk. I put down the little glass, and then I looked up and across the room straight at where I figured her eyes were.

"Nothing," I said.

She took off her hat then, and I found myself looking into the hardest eyes I'd ever seen. They were as cold as ice, and dry ice at that; it was hard to believe they'd ever cried, or looked at anything but bleak and windswept sagebrush desert.

I'd said the wrong thing.

"Sister," she said, "you just said the wrong thing. You come up here, from God knows where—"

"She's from Veedersburg, Indiana," Ol' Pete interrupted. "She never made no secret of that."

I threw him a grateful look, but Renée shook her head.

"From God knows where," she repeated. "You sit in here and drink with us; you follow Buffalo Gal around the woods like a goddamn puppy dog, sucking up everything she knows; you pry, and eavesdrop, and then you go out and harass our cheerleaders; and when I ask you, in a friendly, innocent manner, what you're doing, you say *Nothing?*"

The silence was so thick you could have cut it with a bowie knife. I didn't know what to say. She was right about part of it: I did come in and drink with them, I did ask questions, I did follow Buffy around. But that part about harassing the cheerleaders was way off the mark.

How could I explain that I was doing this for *all* of us?

"All my life," I began, and I prayed my voice wouldn't shake, "there was nothing I wanted more than to be a cheerleader. All through my childhood my parents held up cheerleaders as role models for me. 'My dream,' my dad used to say, 'is that someday you'll be just like them.' We went to every game. And when I watched the professional games on TV—oh, I burned with the desire to be out there with them, leaping and bending and rolling on national television, and flinging my arms out to embrace the whole world!"

I paused for breath. I looked around the room, and I knew I'd struck a chord. No one was saying a word: all eyes were either on me or were dreamy, looking back to their own youthful aspirations, remembering the cheerleaders from all those little towns they'd left—Moab, Ipswich, Findlay, Kennebunk— and I suspected they'd come for much the same reason I had.

I took a deep breath. "I guess it's an old, old story," I went on. "For years I practiced, twirling my baton, getting in shape with tap lessons. I did so many splits that my legs would hardly stay closed. I memorized the chants, the yells, you name it."

They were nodding; they'd been there, too.

"I never made the squad," I said quietly. "Not even the B squad. I just wasn't good enough."

A sigh rippled across the room; some of those dusty eyes were a little damp.

"You know," I said, "there was nothing in the world I wanted more than to be a cheerleader. I would have sold my soul." I laughed softly, sadly. "I guess it's still for sale."

"Hell," Ol' Pete whispered, "so's mine!"

"Whitey," Renée said, standing up and crossing the room to where I stood, "I misjudged you. I'm sorry." She did a forward lunge and stuck out her hand.

I took it. "Renée, Renée, Renée," I said. "You were right about so many things."

She punched me on the arm with her hook. "Howsabout a turn at the cards?" she said.

"Yeah! Yeah!" The crowd roared its approval, and Ol' Pete

actually did a herkie. I grinned with pleasure; this was another Montana tradition. In many a saloon heated discussions came to an end when the cards were pulled out and would-be pugilists resolved their differences with a hand or two of this traditional game of the Old West. It had saved the glassware and bar mirrors of a good many drinking and gaming establishments.

Eight of us sat down around a table, and Ol' Pete dealt the cards. Carol Ann, another shepherd from out at Williston's, held Renée's cards for her—she had trouble managing them with her hook.

It wasn't a long game—these games never are—and one after another the players matched their last card and dropped out. Finally, as fate would have it, Renée and I were face to face. And, friendly as we now were, I was sweating.

I held two cards. Carol Ann was holding one card for Renée, and it was her draw. If she drew the matching card, she'd be out. But if she drew the other, I still had a chance.

Renée kept her eyes on my face and reached. Her hand hesitated above my cards; the tension—friendly tension—in the room was palpable. And then, as Renée's hand descended, she stopped. She lifted her head. "Listen," she said.

I'd heard it, too. A rhythmic clapping, the soft patter of sneaker-shod feet. And then, voices.

"H-O-W-D-Y! Hey-hey! We say Hi!" And through the swinging doors she burst, the first cheerleader the Silver Dollar had ever seen. She popped those doors back and bounced into the room, her hands rolling in front of her, her blond curls cascading over her shoulders. She bounded across the room, right over to our table, and dropped to one knee, one arm flung out to her side and the other straight over her head. "DeeDee!" she cried.

Another cheerleader leaped through the door and sprang over to kneel beside the first. Flinging her arms exactly the same way, she cried, "Kristi!"

And they kept on coming, the doors swinging and banging against the wall, their little rubber-soled feet tap-tapping through the peanut shells that littered the Silver Dollar's floor. "Debbi! Suzi! Lori! Heather! Patti! Mindy! Lisa! Darlene!" They climbed on top of each other till their human pyramid reached the ceiling. They jumped up and landed in splits on the bar.

And in the dim light from the bar we saw that they had changed. Gone were their pleated skirts, the snowy white tennies, the matching panties. Their sweaters were black from the smoke of a thousand campfires and stiff with the arterial blood of dying elk. The dimpled knees were hidden in layers of wool, of heavy-duty twill, of camouflage-pattern neoprene. Their sneakers were gray, worn; their little socks showed through holes in the toes.

And their faces. No longer pink and shiny, their skin was rough from winter winds, wrinkled from the brutal western sun. The blond hair was stringy and sort of greasy, after so long without indoor plumbing.

But their teeth! One after another, they smiled; again and again the gloom of the Silver Dollar was broken as their teeth flashed little reflections of the neon beer signs in the windows. Years of fluoridated water, decay-preventive dentifrices, and orthodonture had done their magic. Whiter than new snow, more uniform than kernels of hybrid corn, brighter than Venus, Jupiter, and Mars in alignment, their teeth alone would have revealed them as the cheerleaders they were.

They stood, and knelt, and sat splayed before us in splendid formation, and then they windmilled their arms and all at once leaped into the air, spreadeagling their limbs toward the four corners of the world, and screamed "Yea! Rah! Team!"

Something warm surged through my body; I looked at Renée, and she was smiling right into my eyes. She reached out and took the card that matched hers.

I was the Old Maid.

The crowd went wild, and the cheerleaders bounced and hugged each other, tears rolling down their leathery cheeks, and they all clustered around Renée and wanted to pat her, and touch her, and have her sign their sneakers. It was Renée's moment of glory.

And I might have felt really bad, if something hadn't happened that warmed my heart all the way to the mitral valve. As everybody pushed over to the bar, the cheerleaders spontaneously stopped, and they all came back and stood around me in a circle, and each one put her left hand on the right shoulder of the next cheerleader. And then they bent their knees, and they stuck out their right hands, and in unison they bobbed up and down, as if they were shaking *my* right hand, and they chanted, "YOU'RE OKAY. YOU'RE ALL RIGHT. YOU PUT UP A DARN GOOD FIGHT! Yea! Rah! Whitey!"

There wasn't a dry eye in the room. "A round on me!" I shouted. And they cheered me again.

In the days that followed, I knew something had changed. I had achieved a goal, a major one, and now—temporarily, anyway—I had nothing to strive for. I was happy, but I felt a little empty, too.

On about Wednesday, I was sitting listlessly in the sun, contemplating the bleak future that stretched ahead of me, when I heard someone coming. I looked around and saw that it was Buffalo Gal, and behind her was Renée.

Buffy got right to the point. "We been huddling," she said. "We want you to stick around."

"I don't know," I said. "I'm not sure I can do this any more."

"Not this," Renée said. "There's an opening on the Williston ranch for another shepherd. Carol Ann's getting hitched."

"I don't know anything about sheep," I said.

"You don't have to," Renée said. "They mill around, and you stand there. Or you sing to 'em, sometimes."

"Surely there's others more qualified," I said.

Renée gazed off at the horizon, and rubbed her hook with her mitten. "The thing is, Whitey," she said, "most of us, we never seen a cheerleader since we been here. It's what we came out here for, and we tried to do everything right, and we waited. But they never came until you got here. It's got us hoping again."

"Hoping?" I said.

Hard-bitten, rugged, dry-eyed as she was, she blushed. "We've started practicing again. It's all we really want, still. And we've realized that, even if we'll never be varsity cheerleaders, we can still do the work, learn the new routines. And who knows? Someday they may need a substitute."

I looked at her. There was something in her face I hadn't seen there before, but I recognized it. It was spirit: team spirit. It's something that's hard to find in the West, in Montana, in the wide-open spaces, where women spend most of their time alone. I thought, maybe that's it. It's not the adulation, the cheering, the popularity that we want; it's team spirit.

"I guess I could learn," I said.

So I stayed. I'm still just an assistant shepherd—sort of on the B team—but I'll tell you something: sheep are the best pep club in the world to practice on. You can be out there in front of them walking on your hands, doing triple back flips, and they don't even look at you. They keep on munching the grass, ripping it out of the ground and chewing it up.

But it's in the nature of sheepherding, and of cheerleading, to stick with it, to keep on trying. You realize how hard the cheerleaders have worked to get where they are. That makes you work harder.

Sometimes, of a summer evening—oh, yes; summer finally came—I'll be out there on the range, practicing in front of my sheep. "Give me a P!" I'll shout, and the only response is from a border collie, who obliges on a nearby fencepost. And then the warm summer wind picks up, just as the sun sets, and the sky is all red and purple and pink, and I hear, from miles away, "Two bits!" And maybe a distant figure cartwheels across a hilltop, silhouetted against the place where the sun just disappeared.

And then, from the east where the sky is already dark, I hear "Four bits!" And I know it's Buffalo Gal, calling down from her lonely vigil up on the mountain. And from up at the ranch house, where Renée is loading up supplies to bring out to us the next morning, comes "Six bits!" And I jump up and shout "A dollar!"

And the next voice is so far away the words aren't quite clear—it's up in high pastureland, where the sheep are chewing grass in the dark, and the little lambs are jumping around, or nursing on their moms, and the dogs are lying in the dust after a hard day, sleeping with one eye open, always on the lookout for coyotes. But we all know it's Ol' Pete, yelling, "If you got spirit, stand up and holler!"

And wherever we are, we leap into the sky, and holler for all we're worth. Down in town they probably think it's thunder, but it's us, practicing, ready for when the snow flies in the fall and the cheerleaders come down from the high mountain passes. We'll be ready to go with them, hunting for the Big Game.

Clearwater and Latissimus

◆

SCHOOL HAD been in session for a couple of weeks when Miss Nancy told us the Siamese twins would be in our class. She said we should be kind. "We want them to feel at home, don't we?" she said. I was in love with Miss Nancy, who was large and flat and had browny gold hair curled up around her face. "We want them to live happy, normal lives." How anyone could expect this is beyond me now, but every six-year-old nodded solemnly, gazing at Miss Nancy's curls as she nodded too.

The next morning the first thing we saw was the double wheelchair, a frightening object in itself, parked at the end of the second row of desks. A colored boy with a huge fore-head sat in it, propped up with pillows, and another one, with a normal-sized head, sat so close they seemed to be hugging each other. This one was grinning, and he had the whitest teeth I had ever seen.

Their names were Clearwater and Latissimus Dorsey, and they were joined at the chest. The doctors said that one heart kept the blood circulating through both bodies, and that it was mostly inside Clearwater. Which was a shame, because Clearwater was the dim one: sweet, always smiling, but he'd never said a word until he was four years old, and that's all that he had now—an occasional word, a phrase, a sigh, a movement of the hands. He was said to have water on the brain, and his head was misshapen; he lay back smiling, weak, perhaps paler than his twin, though they were both chocolate brown, with gleaming black hair.

Latissimus was bright, active, and loud. "I can walk," he said to each child who came in the door. "It's Clearwater who can't. I can walk beside him if I want to." No one answered him. We sat down in our chairs, and tried not to look at the place where the Siamese twins were attached. Binky Pilcher was so nervous he wet his pants. Miss Nancy sent him down to the nurse's office so the nurse could call his mother to bring dry clothes. Nobody laughed at him.

"I wouldn't pee my pants," Latissimus said in a loud voice. "It's Clearwater who never got toilet trained. If I peed my pants it would break my mama's heart."

Barbara Nixon whispered that Latissimus looked like a baby bird, chirping and blinking and looking around. "Clearwater," she said, "is still an egg."

By the end of the week everyone was a Siamese twin. All over the playground children were smushed up against each other's chests, walking sideways, playing Siamese hopscotch, climbing the monkey bars in pairs. After a while someone decided you could be joined anywhere; then people walked around with their big toes together, or their hind ends, or the tops of their heads. Streams of Siamese twins passed down Elm Street on the way home from school, hip to hip, cheek to cheek, knee to knee. Wherever you were joined, though, was the place your heart was. You always shared a heart with your Siamese twin.

At recess Latissimus held center stage, Clearwater smiling beside him. "I am probably a mathematical genius," Latissimus said happily to the table full of first graders. "It's the one thing my mama has to be thankful for." Clearwater clutched his milk carton, sucking the milk up through the straw; from time to time Latissimus gave him a piece of graham cracker. Clearwater, his heavy head against the pillow, couldn't lean forward far enough to pick it up himself.

"What's that?" Barbara asked.

"I can do square roots," Latissimus said. He wiped soggy graham cracker off his brother's face.

"Can't you ever be by yourself?" Jack Turnbull asked.

"Can't you even go to the bathroom by yourself?" Ricky Bob Pugh asked; and no one snickered, because we were dying to find out.

"Nope," said Latissimus. He grinned around the table, showing his exotic pink gums. Suddenly he leaned over and kissed Barbara right on the mouth.

Barbara screamed and wiped her mouth ferociously on her sleeve. Everyone else screamed too.

"First comes love," we chanted. "Then comes marriage." We faltered; it was difficult to imagine Barbara pushing a baby carriage *and* the double wheelchair.

"I kiss anybody who wants it," Latissimus said happily. "I am the Kiss King."

The Venice Kiwanis paid for Latissimus to take a special class in calculus over at the high school, and Mr. Stevens of Wendell Stevens Fine Furniture let Mr. Prince Albert Franklin, the colored man who worked for him, use the delivery truck to drive the twins up there. Every Thursday two of us got to wheel them out the classroom door and down to the front entrance, and wait there with them till Mr. Prince Albert came.

Mr. Prince Albert was the tallest man in town. His legs were like broomsticks, and he towered above us as he stalked down the sidewalk to the door. He was so black he was purple, like mulberries, and your heart just about stopped if he looked at you. "How are these sugarboys?" he said every time. "You have a good day in school?"

"We had music today," Latissimus would tell him. Or, "We did Thanksgiving turkeys."

"Is that so," Mr. Prince Albert would say. Clearwater made his little mewing sounds, and Mr. Prince Albert patted him on the head.

Then he turned to us. "These are your bearers today?" he said, gazing down upon us. "Your servitors of the hour?" We nodded proudly and pushed the chair to the curb where Mr. Prince Albert had put the ramp down from the back of the truck. We pushed it up the ramp, with Mr. Prince Albert giving us a hand, and he lashed it in place with a canvas belt, right behind the driver's seat. "An excellent job," he would say to us in the gloom of the truck. "You will be rewarded hereafter."

And we ran down the ramp, which he pulled up behind us like a drawbridge, and we watched from the sidewalk as they drove away before we went back to the classroom, strangely empty without the Siamese twins.

"I think," my mother said, taking a long drag of her Kent cigarette, "it is a sin."

Auntie Toots leaned over and stuck a new cigarette on the end of my mother's and drew on it till it glowed. On mornings after she'd been there I picked her cigarette butts out of the ashtrays and sucked off the lipstick, pretending I was short-haired and skinny and gorgeous, just like her. "The risk was too great," she said.

"What kind of life can it be?" my mother said. She sounded angry. "They should have been separated at birth."

"Who would have got the heart?" Auntie Toots said. She got up and dropped more ice cubes in their glasses and poured more Scotch.

"That's why LaVonda should have done it then," my mother said. "Before she got attached to them."

"Right," Auntie Toots said. "What if it had been Vera and Birdie? And you had to choose one or the other."

I held my breath; but suddenly they looked up, to where I was joined at the waist to the bannister on the landing. "Who's out of bed?" my mother said sharply.

"Nothing," I said, confused. And after Auntie Toots had gotten me a glass of water, and my mother had tucked me back in, I lay back on my pillow and stared into the dark. My head felt funny; I felt like Clearwater. I imagined my sister, Birdie, beside me, stuck to my chest and breathing asthmatically into my face. I imagined Dr. Wells standing beside us, a carving knife raised over his head.

The Siamese twins were late getting back from Christmas vacation. "I've got my own heart!" Latissimus shouted as they came in the door. They had a new wheelchair; Clearwater was still strapped in among pillows, but the other seat folded up, and Latissimus walked beside his brother, holding onto a bar and pushing the chair himself.

They had been to specialists in Chicago. "Right here," Latissimus said, pointing to where they were joined. "There's *two* hearts, right together. One for each of us." With their sophisticated equipment the big-city doctors had detected a second heartbeat, faint but distinct.

"Does that mean you'll get separated?" Barbara asked. She was Latissimus's girlfriend now, but she still screamed when he kissed her. I hated her; I had fallen out of love with Miss Nancy and into love with Latissimus.

"Maybe," Latissimus said. He leaned over and checked Clearwater's lapbelt. "Look at this chair. I'm supposed to get lots of exercise."

Latissimus not only pushed the new chair, he ran with it, careening down the halls, tearing across the gymnasium floor. He joined in handicap races, with Clearwater as the handicap. When spring came he even played softball with us, under new rules he made up himself: when he was at bat, the pitcher had to be extra-gentle, and when he got a hit, the basemen had to count to seven before throwing the ball, to give him a head start. It was only fair. Latissimus made it sometimes, too, racketing into first base, Clearwater bouncing and screaming in delight.

One day during recess I ran inside to go to the rest room, and Clearwater and Latissimus were just coming out of the boys' room. I was suddenly shy; I had never been alone with them before.

"Hi, Vera," said Latissimus.

"Hi," I said. Up close I could see that his eyelashes were actually curly.

"My heart is getting very strong," he said. He and Clearwater came close to where I stood waiting for them to leave so I could go into the girls' room. "Do you want to feel my heartbeat?"

I could not speak, but he took it as assent, a trait I have since recognized in other men. "Here." He took my hand and placed it on their chest, on the seam where their T-shirts were sewn together. "Can you feel it, Vera?" Latissimus asked, looking anxiously into my eyes. "Can you feel which one is mine?"

"I think so," I whispered. I could feel only heat, the heat from their bodies and from my own hot hand; but it was the first gift a boy had ever offered me, and I didn't want him to be disappointed.

"It's getting very strong," he said again. He reached over and kissed my lips, and he smelled like grass that has sat for a day in the sun. "You can be my girlfriend too," he said, and I smiled at Clearwater, who was smiling at me.

What no one had expected was that as Latissimus got stronger, so did Clearwater. One day Miss Nancy noticed that Clearwater was watching her pointer as she tapped it across the blackboard, pointing at new words. "Why, Latissimus!" she said. "Clearwater is paying attention!"

"Oh, yes, ma'am," Latissimus said. "He pays attention to everything." We all stared at Clearwater, and before our eyes he changed. Or, rather, we saw that he *had* changed. Instead of smiling at anything, now he smiled at *things:* at Miss Nancy's pointer, at the bell for recess, into the eyes of Jill Redenbaugh when she handed him a crayon. He didn't use the crayon, but he looked at it, and he turned it over to look at the other end.

"I believe his color is a little better, too," said Miss Nancy, and then she blushed and said quickly, "He looks so healthy."

It was true: his skin, that used to hold a touch of gray, a hint of *pale*, was dark and shiny, like his twin's.

By the end of the school year Clearwater was sitting up straight and drawing pictures on manila paper while we practiced printing words. He drew the same thing again and again: a big round head with little circle eyes and stick limbs poking out of it. "They look like Clearwater," Jack Turnbull said; but when we laughed and turned to look, we saw it wasn't true any more. Clearwater was filling out. His head used to look huge above his useless little body, his skinny arms and legs; but now his arms were rounded with muscles from reaching for crayons, and his neck was full and sinewy.

Latissimus looked up from the equations he was working on his own paper. "He wears my same size now," he said, and we saw that Clearwater and Latissimus were identical, the same size, the same color, the same bright and chirpy look. If they hadn't been stuck together, if they could have changed sides now and then, we might never have told them apart again.

On the last day of school Latissimus told us that he and Clearwater were moving to Chicago. "Mr. Prince Albert Franklin driving us up in the truck," he said. "Us and our furniture and our mama. She got a new job there."

The only rock 'n' roll station Venice could pick up came from Chicagoland. But none of us had ever been there.

"That's a big city, isn't it, Latissimus?" said Miss Nancy. "It will be different living there."

"We going to school at a university," Latissimus said. "Everybody is smart there."

"Clearwater too?" someone said.

"Might be. Probably." Latissimus grinned.

"We'll miss you, Clearwater and Latissimus," Miss Nancy said. She walked over and hugged them both.

"Will you miss us?" Jack called.

Latissimus leaned his head to one side and shrugged, and Clearwater, grinning, shrugged too. "Might be," Latissimus said. "Mama says we be happier among our own kind."

"I doubt they'll get another girlfriend," Barbara said as we walked home.

"No," I said. "We're it forever." We joined ourselves at the elbow and skipped the rest of the way.

We never saw them again. Auntie Toots heard from someone at work that they were settled in a nice apartment, close enough for Latissimus to walk them to school, and that the doctors were treating them free of charge because they were such an interesting case. But after that the memory of the twins began to fade, and though now and then a pair of children would suddenly be locked together at the knee, or at the ear, no one could remember how the game had started.

So we would never ask about the operation that would separate Clearwater and Latissimus, the operation that made them healthy, normal boys. Clearwater, on his own, learned to draw more realistic people, and to read, and to run; and Latissimus, free at last, ran faster, and slowly lost his aptitude for numbers, and dropped out of high school and lost himself in the streets; and Clearwater became a janitor.

Or the operation that would not succeed. It was Clearwater alone who survived, and who lost the little progress he'd made in his few months with us, and sits now, as we all enter middle age, tied alone in the wheelchair, with a vague dim impression in his feeble mind that once he was connected to something bright and loud, and raced to first base amid cheers.

We never heard. And when they became indistinct, and forgotten, we were left with an impression that had something to do with Latissimus's last words to us: that he and Clearwater would be happy in Chicago, among their own kind. It didn't occur to us that he meant anything besides this: that Chicago was a city of Siamese twins, where everybody had someone who shared his heart.

The Spread of Peace

◆

IF PEACE SPREADS, Heather may lose her job. She's a GS-12, the top rank in her field, but suddenly there's no security. And she's not sure how transferable her skills are; are there civilian jobs for a designer of tactical-weapons defense training systems?

She and Roy are at each other's throats, waiting to hear about Roy's promotion. It's his last chance; if he doesn't make major this time around, he's out. He was ironing his camouflage pants when she left for the airport this morning. "They're so faded," he said angrily as she kissed him. "I hate wearing faded cammies." He would be out in the field with his troops the whole time she was at the convention in Miami.

A couple of years ago she'd hated being apart from Roy, but lately she takes any chance to get out of Utah. She hadn't expected it to be so bad. When Roy got the Salt Lake posting, they'd actually been excited. They'd be close to skiing; and with the lower cost of living, they could have a Jacuzzi.

They do have a Jacuzzi. But what Heather had in mind, really, was one she'd seen at the home of Roy's commanding officer near Big Sur: it was in a glass-enclosed studio perched on a cliff overlooking the Pacific. Heather's Jacuzzi is in the bathroom off the kitchen, and if the walls were glass, she could see the Chanticleer children standing on their deck, staring down at the Bivs' house.

Soon after Heather and Roy moved in, Darla Chanticleer brought over a store-bought poppyseed cake, to welcome them to the neighborhood. She sat chatting with Heather in the kitchen, a pale child clinging to her legs. She was wearing a little button that said, "Christ visited America."

"That's nice," Heather said when conversation flagged. "Sort of a nice thing to think about."

"Isn't it?" Darla said. "It's true, too, that's the nicest part."

"It's not just a metaphor?" Heather said.

"Oh, no," Darla said. "He's been here."

Heather likes the thought of Christ visiting America, dropping in with a poppyseed cake. You'd know who he was by the aura around him—he'd walk through the neighborhood glowing, as if he'd been irradiated. It's a comforting thought: his spotless white robe, not a golden hair out of place.

She walks out of her hotel and finds herself right on the beach. The sun has slipped behind the tallest buildings and shadows are crawling across the sand. If she keeps her head turned toward the ocean, she can almost imagine she's out in nature. She hums lightly and pretends that the voices, the roaring cars, the pounding of passing tapedecks are gulls and wind and the crash of waves.

She looks at her watch. The keynote speech is in an hour. She likes keynote speeches; they're invigorating. But maybe she'll skip this one. Why get all charged up when her job may be down the drain?

She sits down on a bench that's still sunlit and looks out at the water. An elderly woman in shorts carries her high heels through the sand, nodding at whatever she hears on her headset. Half-clothed people of all ages run sweatily back and forth. Some black boys strut past, rap blasting from their radio. Two white girls walk by chewing gum and talking loudly, their shirts sliding off their shoulders.

"Today's young people," Heather says.

"I beg your pardon?" A man comes from behind the bench and looks down at her. "Were you talking to me, Missus?"

"Oh! No," Heather says politely.

"Because I'd have to agree with you," he says. He's an old man, in red plaid shorts. "Know-nothings, all of them. Know-nothings and care-nothings. I tell you, I fear for the world."

Heather has never learned how to avoid these people. The talkers, the restless, the crazy; they come as if she calls them. "I suppose most of them turn out all right," she says.

"I don't think so," the man says, sitting down beside her. "I have to say I believe these fashions are statements of their beliefs, which is they believe in maybe sex, maybe money. Look at the way they play that noise, not a thought about another person who maybe doesn't want to hear it."

"Well, but don't you think it's just youthful rebellion?" Heather says. "Just a phase?"

"Rebellion!" the man says. "How can it be rebellion when there's no thought behind it? Is it a phase I went through? No. I went to work." He looks at her. "You had a rebellion maybe. You did some marches? Sit-ins?"

Heather shakes her head. "I joined the military."

"No!" The man sits up straight. "An attractive woman like you!" He shakes his head. "I have to tell you, you're a very attractive woman, you know what I mean? Don't take me the wrong way. But forty years I drove a cab in New York. I drove Sophia Loren to Idlewild. You're right up there."

"Why, thank you," Heather says. She could hear the key-note speech if she left now.

"Please don't take me wrong," the man says. "I'm not try-ing to pick you up. I've got a son; he won't give me the time of day, so the world is my family. You know what I mean? I take an interest."

Heather looks at her watch.

"You want me to get lost, say so," he says. "But I like

people. I thought I'd be happy to retire, leave the cab. But I got lonely. So I took it up again here, part-time." He stands up and holds out his hand. "Hentoff," he says. "Harry Hentoff. Not related to any Hentoffs you ever heard of."

"I'm Heather Biv," says Heather.

"A lovely name for a lovely lady," Harry says, shaking her hand. He sits again. "Biv? That's your husband's name?"

"Short for Bivlovitz," Heather says. "They lost it in transit."

"We all lost something in transit," Harry says. "Everybody's a nobody here. All this talk about roots, who's got roots? Nuclear families!" He waves his hands wildly. "No wonder they fall apart; they're named after a bomb!"

Heather laughs. "I think they're two different things," she says.

"That's what they want us to think," Harry says. He looks at his hands and folds them in his lap. "It may be coincidence, Mrs. Biv, but I've seen too many coincidences to trust them any more. How old are you?"

"Thirty-five," Heather says.

"Hah! A baby." Harry leans forward. "How old do you think I am? Come on, take a guess. How old?"

Heather looks carefully at his face. It's lined and grainy, rough-looking under the tan, but his eyes bore into hers like the eyes of a middle-aged man. "Sixty-five?"

"Hah!" Harry says. "Taxi drivers don't retire on the dot like a businessman. I drove full-time till I was seventy-two. I been here three years. Seventy-five." He nods, smirking. "Seventy-five years old and perfect health."

"I never would have guessed," Heather says, though, really, she might have.

"Old enough to be your grandfather, if there'd been some fast work," Harry says. "Think of it. We could be related."

Three white-haired women walk slowly past, talking loudly. They look at Heather and Harry and then at each other.

"They come here to die," Harry says. "A town full of dying Jews. You're not from here, are you? I got to say, you don't look Jewish."

"No," Heather says. "I live in Utah."

Harry sighs. "I'm a Jew," he says. "I've come here to die, too."

The sinking sun has turned the sand a dark rose color, and a breeze makes its way through the palms and across the sidewalk to the beach. Roy, bivouacked with twenty men in the west desert, would probably kill for such a breeze. Why Utah? Heather thinks for the hundredth time. Why not Florida? Think of the survival skills those boys would learn camped in Miami. She pictures the clot of men in fatigues, bayonets at the ready, watching the dying Jewish ladies trudge through the sand.

"You're on vacation?" Harry says.

She shakes her head. "Business. I'm supposed to be in a meeting right now."

"Traveling for business!" Harry says. "What business are you in?"

"I work for the armed services," she says. "Systems design."

"Computers," he says. "I knew you were a smartie. That's where to be these days." He nods. "You know when the first computers came out? The nineteen-fifties. I was already driving the cab. I put my son through college and then through medical school, all from the cab. I had regular customers; they always asked for me. 'Give me Harry Hentoff,' they'd say. Any children?"

"No," Heather says.

"They're not necessary. Zero population growth is what we need. That's what I did, just the one. I did my part to save the world and what do I get? He doesn't have time to call me. It's okay; I don't like him much anyway."

"I'd like to have one," Heather says. "Someday."

"Look at that tanker," Harry says. "It's probably Russian.

They pick up oil in Siberia and run it to Cuba. They take care of their own, no matter what you might think." They watch the tanker, a rigid shape against the brighter sky. "This *glasnost*, it might not be such a good thing. I won't say their system's perfect. But maybe they're giving up too early."

"The people seem to want it," Heather says.

"Who knows?" Harry says. "We hear what the capitalist press tells us. What do we know goes on in the hearts of the people?"

"Do you think that?" Heather says. "That the press lies?"

"All I'm saying, people hear what they want to hear, the papers no different. There's a problem in the Soviet Union, they blame it on communism. They see the same problem here, who do they blame?" He looks slyly at Heather. "Communists!" He slaps his thigh. "I have to tell you this," he says. "I've been a communist for fifty-five years."

"Funny, you don't look communist," Heather says.

"You have a sense of humor, for someone in the military," Harry says.

"I'm not really in it," Heather says. "I just work for them. I flunked officer training."

"A smartie like you!" Harry says. "That's why the government runs into trouble, they flunk someone like you. Why?"

"I fainted on the obstacle course," Heather says.

"For that they flunk you?"

"What if all the officers had fainted in Vietnam?" Heather says.

"We would of been out of there toot sweet, believe it, Missus," Harry says. "But you work for them anyway?"

"It's a good job," Heather says. "My husband's an officer. Not too many civilian jobs would transfer me every time he gets a new posting."

"They think of all the angles, don't they," Harry says. "They got you by the balls. Pardon my French. Anyway, this *perestroika*. These things might be good, but I'm not convinced. I got to tell you, maybe it's not my business, but I feel betrayed. I don't think they gave the system a chance."

"They had seventy years," Heather says. But that's how she feels, too. Betrayed by peace.

"It's not something I'm proud of," Harry says. "But they change the system on you; it's what they call a paradigm shift. All of a sudden, your life is for nothing any more."

That's it, Heather thinks. Sitting beside Harry Hentoff in Miami, watching a Russian tanker on its way to Cuba, surrounded by people who might as well be from other planets, Heather thinks, It's not my job, it's not Roy, it's not even Utah. It's a paradigm shift. "I don't think I've ever met a communist before," she says.

Harry grins. "See what I mean? All your life they warn you against commies, and who the hell do they turn out to be? Me. A poor cabbie."

"But how did you get to be one?"

"I don't mean to disparage your career," Harry says, glancing at her, "but I just never fell for all the claptrap. Don't get me wrong, the U.S.A. is the greatest country on earth. I sincerely believe that. But it would be even greater if it were communist."

"Isn't that claptrap too?" Heather says. "Just going from one extreme to the other?"

"Now you're thinking," Harry says. "All I mean is, we got two of the greatest countries in the world, and if we could bring them together, who could beat us? Free speech under a communist government. We'd have it made in the shade. Of course, it'd mean big cutbacks in defense. You and your husband would be out of work."

"We'll probably be out of work anyway," Heather says. "But Roy's always wanted to run a garden center."

"A garden center?" Harry laughs. "See, I got them too. A thousand preconceptions. What about you? I know. You'd have that baby."

Heather sighs. "I can't decide."

"What's to decide?" Harry says. "It's normal. Women have babies. As old as Adam and Eve. Why not?"

"I might be too old," Heather says. "I might die before it grows up."

Harry shakes his head. "I won't argue with you," he says. "I won't mention car wrecks or botulism or the atom bomb. My wife was forty when our son was born. In those days it was like fifty. She's older than I am, but she looks like a young woman. I told someone once, in fact it was someone in government, naming no names, I told him, 'Letty's five years older than I am,' and he said, 'Harry, I don't believe it. I would have said ten years younger.' You think she was pleased to hear that? No. I tell her Ira Magaziner thinks she looks sixty, she gets mad, she says why did I tell him her age? She's a difficult woman. I wouldn't wish her on my worst enemy. I look forward to dying so I'll finally be free."

"The Mormons believe families will be together for eternity," Heather says.

"Thank God I'm an atheist," Harry says. "You're a Mormon?"

"No," Heather says. "I was raised Catholic, but I'm nothing now."

"Religion has never attracted me," Harry says. "All this hoopla over something that happened in some desert."

"The Mormons believe that Christ visited America," Heather says. "They think the Indians are the lost tribe of Israel."

"That doesn't surprise me," Harry says. "People who believe in Jesus Christ will believe anything."

They sit looking out to sea. It is completely dark now, but the beach still shudders with the shrieks of teenagers, and the street behind them is loud with people looking for a good time.

"The thing is," Heather says, "I think I have cancer." There. She has said it aloud.

"I had cancer," Harry says. "Twenty years ago. What kind do you have?"

"A lump in my breast." Heather feels dizzy saying it.

"Have you been to the doctor?"

"No. I just found it this morning."

"This isn't something you wait around," Harry says.

"I'll go when I get home," Heather says. "It's just, I'm kind of scared."

"They do amazing things with lumps," Harry says.

"I know," Heather says.

"I was a young man of fifty-five when one of my testicles swelled up the size of a navel orange," Harry says. "Maybe a small grapefruit. Letty thought I'd been abusing myself. 'You spend so much time in the bathroom, now I know why,' she yells. 'It's got nothing to do with it,' I tell her, 'I spend a lot of time because of my business.' The Lebanese were moving into the taxi field. Competition. A man who was clean shaven and smelled good, who didn't have hair growing out his ears, had an advantage. Letty's an unsophisticated woman."

"What happened to your testicle?" Heather says.

"I walked like I had a hard-on," Harry says. "Women crossed the street, all they could see was the bulge in my trousers. Me who was never unfaithful to Letty, hardly. Let me tell you, I was at the clinic that same day. Something like a testicle, a breast, you don't take it lightly."

"No," Heather says. "It's part of who you are."

"Damn right," Harry says. "They sliced my ball off the next day. Now I only got one, but it works as good as two. Better, it tries harder."

"But you were okay?" Heather says. "The cancer didn't come back?"

"Never," Harry says. "The doctors said to keep an eye on it. Every morning I shove my hand up there, poke around for lumps. Nothing. Not even prostate trouble. My son says, Dad, be careful, watch it close. What does he know. He may be a doctor, but what does he know about his father's testicles?"

"I don't know," Heather says.

"Do you believe in fate?" Harry says. "Do you think there's a reason I just at that moment walked by and heard you talking to yourself, just the day you find a lump in your breast?"

"I thought you didn't believe in God," Heather says. "I thought you weren't religious."

"I'm not talking religious," Harry says. "What god is going to send me walking down the beach with split-second timing? I mean fate. It's more of a man-made thing."

"I don't think I believe in it," Heather says. "I think things just happen."

"Exactly," Harry says. "It just so happens that I know something about lumps in the breast. My wife never touched her own breasts; the thought of it made her faint. Imagine! But we never gave it a thought; it didn't occur. Breasts were made to be covered up. Not like today; they don't cover anything. So our son marries a nurse, and what's the first thing she says to my wife? Touch yourself, she says. Every month, you got to examine your breasts or you'll die.

"Letty doesn't want her in the house. 'Don't bring her here,' she tells him, but he don't listen; he's a good boy. Next thing you know, Toni, that's her name—an Italian Catholic which let me tell you doesn't go over big either—Toni brings over this box of fake breasts. Falsies! Letty could of died. She won't look anyplace but out the window. So Toni shows me how to do it. Palpate the tissue, check out the nodes. Quadrant by quadrant. Feel this. Feel that."

He shakes his head. "It's a new age," he says, "sitting there with your daughter-in-law telling you how to feel up imitation breasts while your wife looks out the window. But here's the thing. There was five of them, all different shapes and sizes, and they had different lumps. Some of them bobble around under your fingers, and some of them feel attached, and some of them are as hard as marbles. All different. I don't know if you know this, but some women's breasts are always lumpy. All the time. Cystic. Nothing wrong with them; they're just full of little knots. Perfectly healthy. You got breasts like that?"

"I don't know," Heather says.

"They're tricky," Harry says. "But what I'm getting to is this. Every month I do it to Letty. She don't let on, she doesn't want to talk about it, but every month I check for lumps. Fifteen years, what's that? A hundred and eighty times, I check her breasts. A hundred and ninety, sometimes I cop an extra. Twice I found lumps. 'Letty,' I tell her, 'go to the clinic.' She goes, she gets a test. Each time a cyst."

He sits up straight and takes Heather's hand before she can pull it away. "Missus," he says, "I can do this for you. You're attractive, yes, to be honest I have to say I'd like to touch your breasts in the other way. But you don't have to worry with me, I do it because of my interest in people. Also, my son's a doctor. So I know."

"Mr. Hentoff," Heather says.

"Harry," he says.

"Harry. It's very kind of you to offer, but I couldn't do that."

He sighs. "I suppose not." They watch the running lights of a sailboat coming in to shore. "Just tell me one thing," he says. "Does it feel attached? Or does it bobble?"

Heather's face feels hot. She hasn't been so embarrassed in years—not because of their discussion, but because she doesn't know if her lump bobbles. She doesn't even know if her breasts are naturally lumpy. In the darkness she puts her hand down her shirt and presses the top of her breast, where the lump is. She can't tell; she has nothing to compare it to. "Here," she whispers. She guides Harry's hand to where the lump is. "Do you feel it?"

"I think so," he whispers. He's twisted toward her, his face close to hers, but his eyes gaze at something above and behind her. "If you put your hand behind your head," he says. With his free hand he lifts hers and pats it into place. "I think they're sort of cystic," he says. "Definitely cystic. I can feel the one you're worried about." His fingers move in little circles around the edges of her breast, pressing lightly. "Upper left quadrant. What you got is I think a cyst. Nothing to worry about." His hand moves to the upper right quadrant. "Very cystic."

"But nothing to worry about?"

"Well, remember, I'm not a doctor. I got my training on the job, so to speak. But in my experience, I think it's okay. Go to the doctor when you get home." His fingers inch toward the lower right quadrant. "You want I should do the whole thing? Both maybe? Two for the price of one, hah!"

"No thank you," Heather says. "Just the one. I was nervous about it."

"Glad to be of help," Harry says. He withdraws his hand from her shirt and looks at it. "You got nice breasts, Missus," he says. "Your husband's a lucky man."

"Thank you," Heather says. "Does it . . . do you notice any difference? I mean, between cystic breasts and the others."

"Each one is unique," Harry says. "But you mean in attractiveness. No. Just different. You're attracted to a woman, you're attracted to all of her. I don't suppose you want to examine my prostate." He sighs. "No, I guess not. Not a laughing matter."

Back in Utah, Heather gets out of the Jacuzzi and goes outside. She pulls out the chaise and lies down on her stomach, letting her arms drop on either side. Her nose is squashed into the terry cloth. Maybe, she thinks, I should rewrite my résumé. Now. Just in case.

"Hi there, neighbor!" It's Darla Chanticleer, surrounded by children. "Getting some sun?"

"Sure am," Heather says, squinting up at her.

"Say, Heather," says Darla, "I don't know how much you know about our church?" She pauses, but not for long; she knows Heather knows almost nothing. "But we collect newspapers? The first Saturday of every month."

"Newspapers?" Heather says.

Darla nods happily. "Just bundle them up and leave them on the curb. The young women I work with will pick them up."

"Newspapers," Heather says. "Oh, was that the phone?" She jumps up, and has to lean over to keep from passing out. When she straightens up, Darla and the children are watching closely. "Well, see you," Heather says.

"Bye now," Darla says.

"Have a nice day, Mrs. Biv," says a child.

Heather can't decide what to do this weekend. Roy and his men are conducting actual battle simulations in the foothills, and he won't be home until tomorrow night, grimy, sweaty, full of adrenaline.

Roy has been passed over for promotion again. At the end of this year he will be honorably discharged, with full retirement benefits. Heather has never known Roy when he wasn't an officer. It's part of what she loves about him: she's proud of his devotion to his principles, his decisiveness, the way he shines his shoes. When she married him she knew she was marrying the military. It hasn't been easy, but it was her choice. Now he'll be just her husband—a whole paradigm shift.

Last night Heather heard the explosions of artillery, and the house actually shook. "It's a fairly unique weather situation," a Major Grimwald said on the news. "Clouds over the Salt Lake Valley reflected the noise and vibration of our self-propelled howitzers right into some city neighborhoods." He looked sternly into the TV camera. "We've never had this problem before."

Even the weather is different, Heather thinks. Maybe their new life, the post-military life they talk about more and more these days, will be better, a dream come true. Roy has started looking into business schools and landscape-design programs; the mail is full of catalogs with cover photos of coeds strolling past ivy-covered buildings. Roy is taking it well, plunging right into civilian life. It'll be a different sort of thing, won't it? Running a garden center is sort of a vote for peace.

She goes for a drive. Out on the highway, west of the city, she puts the top down and presses on the accelerator. That's one thing Utah's good for, anyway: traveling the interstate at high speed, the wind ripping her hair back from her face, the sun coating her arms, the cops speeding the other way, waving as they pass. Heather touches the lump; it's smaller. It's changing, going away.

She wrote Harry a letter after she'd been to the Breast Care Center. "Dear Mr. Hentoff," she started, but she threw that away. "Dear Harry," she began again.

> I took your advice and went to the doctor, who
> sent me for a mammogram. As you suspected, my
> lump is probably a simple fatty tumor, a lipoma,
> which is common in fibrocystic breasts like mine.
> I need to keep an eye on it, but so far my breasts
> remain untouched.

She thought Harry would appreciate that bit of humor, and she sent the letter to the address he'd written on the back of one of her business cards. But in the envelope that came from Miami the next week was her own letter, torn in half, with FILTH! written across it in purple ink.

On the day her meeting ends, Harry is waiting for her in the hotel lobby. He carries her bags out to where his cab is parked. "So how was it?" he says.

"Pretty good," Heather says. "There may be a place for me in the private sector."

Harry nods, looking at her in the rearview mirror. He looks older in daylight, his skin more lined, his forehead spotty. "Computers," he says. "The wave of the future." He drives them up the ramp onto the expressway. "You know, it's not so bad down here. All my wife's pals, they're all here. Gives her something to do."

They drive for a while, and then he turns off the highway onto a smaller road, and then onto a sandy track. "I want to show you this," he says. "Don't worry, we have plenty of time."

Pools of water start to appear beside the road, and finally they are driving along a jetty at the edge of the sea. It ends at a narrow, sandy beach, and Harry stops the car. They get out and walk across the sand. The water is dark, and the air is heavy with the smell of fish and diesel fuel; gulls scream overhead.

"Look." Harry points toward a clump of mangroves out in the water.

"What?" Heather says.

"Look close," he says. "In the trees."

Suddenly she sees that the treetops are full of pink birds, their heads poking up above the leaves. There are dozens of them, and she realizes that what she thought was the noise of the city is a great commotion of squawks drifting across the water.

"Spoonbills," Harry says. "Roseate spoonbills. I bet you never saw them before."

Heather shakes her head.

"Me neither," he says. "I never even heard of them before I moved down here to die. You wouldn't think big birds like that could live in trees, like regular birds, would you?"

They gaze at the roseate spoonbills.

"This is a beautiful place," Heather says.

"I found it myself," Harry says. "Just driving around. I've never seen one other person here." He waves his arm toward the water. "So close to the city, so close to the airport. Sometimes I just come out here to sit and look at the water."

"It's so peaceful," Heather says.

"But," Harry says, "we have a plane to catch."

When they reach the airport and pull up in front of the terminal, Harry turns around to look at her, hooking his arm over the back of the seat. "My son had a vasectomy," he says. "'Pop,' he tells me, 'I don't want to bring a child into this world. There's no hope.' 'No hope?' I said. 'Children are the only hope.' But it's too late, he's had himself neutered. Maybe he's right. What's the point? Just to make old men happy, young men should make babies? Letty says it's my fault, I never gave him his bar mitzvah. She says it's a judgment, my son doesn't respect life. I don't know. I did what I thought was right." He shrugs, and shakes his head. "So are you going to have that baby? You and your husband?"

"I don't know," Heather says. "There's so many other things we want to do."

"Either way," he says, "I think you'll be fine."

He gets her suitcase from the trunk and sets it on the sidewalk, and they shake hands. Heather picks up her bags and is swept into the terminal in the crowd of people. When she turns to look back, Harry is standing on the sidewalk, watching her. She waves, and he gives her a thumbs-up sign. Then he cups his hands around his mouth and shouts, "Nothing but heartache they bring. But what else do we live for?"

But a large group of people, all speaking loudly in Spanish, has moved between them, and Heather's not sure that she heard him correctly. She shrugs, and it seems to be the right response because Harry shrugs too, and grins. With a last wave he turns back toward the cab. She stands still as people push past, watching Harry's pink head disappear in the crowd, and wonders if she heard him right. It will give her something to think about all the way home.

The Kidnappee

◆

BENNY SARVER knows what's going on in the lab where they clone babies out of one-eyed frogs. He and JacQuelle snuck in there one night and looked in all the incubators. JacQuelle wants to take one home, raise it in the microwave turned on low, but they didn't find any that time. "Nothing de*vel*oped enough," is what JacQuelle says.

Of all the floors he works, the fourth is Benny's favorite. Free time, he goes up there and has a smoke in the custodial closet. He thinks about the one-eyed frog babies all the time. What color do they turn out? He wishes he could get one for JacQuelle.

"Cindy better look out," Benny says over supper at home. "Nobody think anything come of it, but Cindy better just look out."

"Keep her pants on," JacQuelle says.

"I don't know about that," Benny says.

"I don't blame her none, with Harvey for a husband, but I can't imagine doing it with a Chinese," JacQuelle says.

"What a racist thing," Benny says. "What about Billy? What about Mohammed Yin?"

"They no more Chinese than you are African," JacQuelle says. "I mean aboriginal Chinese. They are so small."

"Cindy is a delicate woman," Benny says. "She smaller than she look. Anyway, she is naive."

"That's for sure," JacQuelle says.

"Why don't you talk to her?" Benny says. "Maybe she open up to you."

"What, I walk up and say Cindy baby, I hear you making it with John Chin? He any good?"

"I'm worried about her," Benny says. "She might be making the wrong plans."

JacQuelle sighs. "She so naive," she says. "I feel like her mother."

"Stop by," Benny says.

When John Chin lifts the toilet seat he yelps and jumps back. I LOVE YOU is written on the underside in blood. He steps closer and sees that it isn't blood, it's lipstick. So graffiti is a means of personal communication, he thinks, in addition to being a method for political and social commentary? He is unsure of the proper behavior in this case. Should he remove it? Leave a message in its place? He wipes at it with toilet tissue, but the message stays, blurred but legible. "Oh dear," John Chin says.

Benny has seen them come and go. He can tell the smart ones the first day, by their faces, like squirrels, popping their eyes around. They're usually Asian and they don't stay long. A year, two years, picking up techniques, sucking up knowledge like a wet-vac, then off to the next place. Benny sees them radiating out from the fourth floor of his wing, all over the country. He is the hub of a nation of Asian scientists.

"I ever find us one of them frog babies, I hope it's got Asian cells," he says to JacQuelle.

"A jumping Jap baby?" she says. "Korean croaker? Libbit, libbit?"

Lord, she is lacking in respect. But funny. She keeps him smiling.

Cindy assures John Chin it's not an American love custom. "When I got kidnapped?" she says. "That's how they found me. Lipstick on toilet seats, all across Iowa."

John Chin thinks Cindy is the most beautiful woman he has ever seen. When she first took off her glasses she reminded him of a loyal animal. "We could go there sometime," he says.

"Iowa?" Cindy says.

"You could show me these toilet seats," he whispers, leaning toward her.

What happened was this: she walks out of Kroger's, the butter and a peach lipstick in a sack, and opens the door of her father's new Mustang. Two men come up behind her. "Hop in, Ginger," one says. "I'll drive." Cindy hands over the keys and gets into the backseat.

Once, near Indianapolis, she says, "Where are we going?"

"Ha, ha," the driver says. "Why don't you get some sleep?"

She doesn't, but she doesn't do anything else, either. She watches the fields of corn stubble fly by until it gets dark, and then she leans back and stares out the back window at the Big Dipper. She stops thinking. She just stops.

It seems to her that she has never started up again. She lives a normal life—goes to college, gets married, has children—but when she looks back, she can't remember actually doing anything.

Until now. Lying beside John Chin as his room darkens in the late afternoon, she thinks marrying John Chin would be like voting in favor of a new world order. It would be taking significant action on a personal level, casting off the closed-minded parochialism of Harvey and her parents and furthering world peace and international biotechnical development. When John Chin wins the Nobel Prize, she, Cindy Gooldy Butter Chin, will be beside him.

JacQuelle comes up to the cloning wing on Wednesday. "I can't stay long," she says. "You smoking in here?"

"It's the only place I smoke," Benny says. "You got no jurisdiction."

"If you saw what I see," she says. She's an X-ray tech down on first south. She brings home some of the worst lungs and hangs them on the refrigerator, just to scare him. "Where's Cindy at?"

He leads her down toward the biochem department office and JacQuelle screeches to a stop as they pass the open door, as if she's taken by surprise. "Why Cindy!" she says. "How *are* you?"

"Hi, JacQuelle," Cindy says.

"You looking a little peaked," JacQuelle says. "Cindy, you all right? You working too hard?"

Like a charm, Benny thinks. JacQuelle has a talent for it. Cindy's little blue eyes fill up just like that. A little sympathy is all it takes, a personal concern. The world could take a lesson from JacQuelle.

"Cindy, honey, you come in the powder room with me," JacQuelle says, all warm and quiet. "You take your break and come on."

And there's a flurry, Cindy scooting her chair back and trying to hide her face, JacQuelle spreading her wings in protection, and off they fly to the ladies' room. Benny goes and gets an OUT OF ORDER sign from the closet and hangs it on the door.

"I don't know what to do," Cindy says. "Nothing like this has ever happened to me."

JacQuelle sits down on the radiator and fluffs her hair. "This John Chin?" she says.

Cindy stares at her. "How do you know?"

"Honey, it's common knowledge," JacQuelle says. "It a small world."

"Oh my God," Cindy says.

"Look, nobody going to tell Harvey," JacQuelle says. "Nobody going to tell anyone. But if you in love, you shouldn't be sitting there looking like a ghost. That is the indication that something is wrong."

"I've never felt like this," Cindy says. "I never knew what happiness was."

"Look like you still don't," JacQuelle says.

"He's so different from Harvey! He listens to me. He understands me. We're so much alike."

"Two peas," JacQuelle says.

"I feel good with him. I feel like I've finally found what to do with my life. It's like we're partners, two of us against the world."

JacQuelle gets out her nail file. "That's nice. Now John Chin's young, isn't he?"

"The age difference doesn't bother us!" Cindy says. "We don't even notice it, not since the first time. He wants to marry me."

"Huh," JacQuelle says. "You going to do it?"

"I don't know," Cindy says solemnly. "I honestly don't know. It would be the most important thing I've ever done in my life."

"This have an impact on your family," JacQuelle says.

"I know," Cindy says. "I think the girls would adjust. Really. I just wish . . . "

JacQuelle waits.

"I just wish I hadn't had Philip yet," Cindy says. She stares at her reflection. "I wish he could have been John's child."

"Libbit," JacQuelle says. "John want kids?"

"He says Science is his child," Cindy says.

"I see," says JacQuelle.

"Benny?" John Chin knocks at the door of the supply closet.

Benny looks out. "What you need, Johnny?" he says.

John Chin likes Benny very much. No one else calls him Johnny, which is the familiar diminutive of the Americanized version of his real name. "Benny, you are expert in sanitary engineering?"

"You tickle the hell out of me, Johnny," Benny says. "You can just call me a janitor."

"The directory says this," John Chin says. "In any case, I have a question about lipstick."

"Don't wear it," Benny says. "I don't think it convey the impression you after, Johnny."

John Chin thinks this is hilarious. "Quite a joke," he says. "No, I need to remove it from a bathroom fixture."

"Oh, you mean Cindy," Benny says. "Ammonia. Ammonia clean anything. Keep a jug of it in the home at all times."

"Ah," John Chin says. "Yes, that's great. Thank you, Benny. Hey, working hard today or hardly working?"

"Keeping an eye on things," Benny says.

Cindy's mom keeps all the clippings and puts them in a scrapbook. Cindy and her brother like to read their favorite parts aloud.

> "She just went to Kroger's for some butter," a
> distraught Mrs. Gooldy sobbed.

They shout the best sentences in unison.

> But for Cindy it was to be a long, strange trip
> she would never forget!

"Oh, how can you children laugh?" Mrs. Gooldy says.

"It's okay, Mom," Cindy's brother says. "Don't get distraught."

Willie G.'s on jury duty, so Benny subs for him. Benny thinks that if Willie G. wasn't so overloaded with civic and familial duty he'd probably move into the animal wing, get himself a big nesting box somewhere in a mouse room.

Willie G. calls him up to give him instructions. "You got to be sterile before you go in," he tells Benny. "Just one speck of alien substance can wipe out a whole colony."

"I am one hundred percent sterile," Benny says. "I been tested."

"This is no joke, Benny," Willie G. yells. "You got millions of research dollars riding on your shoulders."

Benny's done it before. He showers in the little cubicles between rooms, suits up in scrubs and paper shoes, ties the face mask on. He empties trash and mops floors in mouse rooms, rat rooms, rabbit rooms. All those little pink eyes staring at him give him the creeps. No sound but rodents rustling around in their wood shavings, and the flap of his mop. Nighttime they don't even have the radio playing over the loudspeakers.

In the herp lab he slows down, looks in all the tanks. Big old African bullfrogs, warty and striped, look back at him from half underwater. They probably wish they were back in Africa, lying in a swamp, breeding the natural way.

Benny puts his face down close to one tank, even with one of the frogs, and looks into its one big eye. It's a funny eye, like a cat's, just a little slit to look through. A skin slides over it.

"*Chura*," Benny says. That means frog in Swahili, a language Benny has studied. He likes the sound of it; it would make a good name. "*Chura*," he says.

The kidnappers stop at a gas station. When Cindy comes out of the ladies' room and gets into the backseat, the short kidnapper turns around. "Nice car," he says. "Where'd you pick it up?"

"It's my dad's," Cindy says.

"Sure," says the man. "No, really. Is it yours?"

Cindy looks at him.

The tall kidnapper starts the engine. "Rick find it somewhere?"

"Rick?" says Cindy.

"Are you on something?" the tall one says.

"On something?" Cindy says.

"Snap out of it," the short one says. He leans toward her, half smiling. "You are Ginger, aren't you?"

"I thought you were Ginger," Cindy says.

The man looks at the driver. "I don't get it," he says. "Louis here will tell you I'm not big on jokes."

Cindy feels her heart lurch into action, as if it hasn't beaten since she came out of Kroger's. "Honest," she says. "I thought he called you Ginger."

The driver turns all the way around. "Didn't Rick set this up? Didn't he tell you we needed a lift to Denver?"

"Denver?" says Cindy.

"Denver! Denver!" says the short man. "Where the hell else would we be going?"

"I don't know any Rick," Cindy says.

"Are you Ginger or not?" the driver says.

"I'm Cindy Gooldy," Cindy says. "I've never been west of the Mississippi."

The tall kidnapper stares at her. "Why didn't you say something?"

"What would I say?" Cindy says. "I thought you knew what you were doing."

"It's nutritious," Philip tells her, finishing up a box of cornstarch.

It must be something they learn in nursery school, she thinks. That's the problem with her whole life. She always thinks everyone else knows what they're doing.

"You know, they feed them cornstarch now," she says casually to Harvey, who spins around to look at Philip lying motionless in front of the television.

"You let him eat it?" he says. "You let him eat a box of cornstarch?"

"Benny?" John Chin's at Benny's door again. "Benny, I need to consult you."

Benny pushes open the door and grinds out his cigarette in a dustpan. "Shoot, J.C.," he says.

"This may be a violation of a sacred trust," John says. His pursed lips make him look like a chipmunk.

"I am the soul of discretion," Benny says. He reaches for John's shoulder and pulls him into the closet. He shuts the door and flips on the light. "What's going down, Johnny?"

John Chin pulls an envelope from his shirt pocket. "I need a translation," he says. He takes a Polaroid picture from the envelope and hands it to Benny. "An interpretation. Can you explain this to me, please?"

Benny looks at it. It's a picture of a toilet with its seat up. "You mean the words?"

John nods.

"Cindy times John?" Benny looks from the photo to John Chin's blank face. "That what you mean?"

"What is this symbol, please?" John says.

"The times?" Benny says. "That just mean love. Cindy times John. Two times two."

"Ah, of course," John Chin says. "Love."

Benny hands the photo back. "You got any plans about that?"

John Chin tucks the picture back into the envelope and shakes his head. "I cannot make plans. It is Cindy who has major family responsibilities."

Benny nods. He hands John Chin a cigarette and they smoke for a while. "She know you're going to Baltimore?"

"Yes," John Chin says. "I have asked her to come with me. I have laid it on the line, Benny."

Benny looks at him for a minute. "I wonder if you know this one thing about Cindy," he says. "When she got kidnapped?"

John nods.

"She didn't leave no lipstick notes," Benny says. "One of them kidnappers did it, to help her out."

John Chin leans back against the clean towels, tapping his cigarette gently on the back of his hand. He stares at a carton of rubber gloves. "Ah," he says.

JacQuelle leans forward, looking into the mirror, and fills in the outline she made around her mouth with bright red lipstick. "You ever getting up?" she says.

Benny rolls over. "I'm up," he says. He puts on his glasses. "You going before the lord dressed like that?"

"Ain't no action here," JacQuelle says. "I got a solo today."

Benny goes to the window to watch her come out the front door down below. She marches along Dorchester, headed for Calvary. JacQuelle is not the most religious woman he has ever known, but she has the voice of an angel.

Philip's small fingers have smeared the lipstick, but the message can still be read. WASH YOUR HANDS AFTER YOU FLUSH, it says. Harvey takes a plastic squeeze bottle from under the sink and puts some ammonia on a sponge. He carefully wipes the toilet seat clean.

Harvey is supposed to solo with the choir this morning, but he drops the girls off at church and keeps driving. He imagines JacQuelle finishing her part, and then the organ prelude leading to his; and then silence. The congregation gets restless, and the choir looks around, craning their necks, shifting and muttering. The organ repeats the lead-in, and then JacQuelle stands up again and sings his part in her high sweet voice.

He parks the car and walks into the zoo. The air is still wet with remnants of nighttime. It's so early nobody's here yet, just Harvey and some bag people. Two ladies are sitting on a bench in front of the reptile house, looking into each other's bags. The shopping-cart man is settling down for a snooze up in the sea lion bleachers, his cart parked in the bushes below.

Harvey has turned forty, and he's happy about it. He feels good; he's leaving so much behind. He doesn't know what's next, but he's optimistic.

He walks past the sea lions and stops beside the kangaroos, where a mother kangaroo is lying like an odalisque in a patch of sun while her joey hops happily about. Harvey watches it hop to the edge of the moat around the pen and peer over. It topples in.

The joey goes under. Harvey looks around wildly for a keeper, but there are no zoo people in sight. The shopping-cart man is standing in the bleachers, his hands cupped around his mouth. "Save it!" he's shouting.

Harvey climbs over the railing and sits on the high edge of the moat. It's a ten-foot drop, but it's on an incline, and he knows he'd better not think. He leans backward, slips off the edge, and slides down, shredding the skin on his elbows. He crashes into the water. It's only a couple of feet deep, and he plunges over to where the joey has stopped struggling. He picks it up. It's smaller than Philip, but its tail is heavy. It lies still and limp in his arms. The mother kangaroo is growling above him.

He wants to push the water out of the joey's lungs, but there's no place to lay it flat, so he turns it upside down. Holding it by its bunchy thighs he shakes it, and sure enough, with every jerk water spurts from the joey's mouth. He shakes it again and again, and, holding it like a baby, he puts his mouth over the joey's muzzle and blows. He blows again. He can feel the little chest expand, and contract, and then the joey shudders with its own breath.

People are cheering. Standing in the water Harvey looks up, and above him the mother kangaroo is leaning over, her paws clasped to her chest. Across from her the shopping-cart man has appeared, laughing and cheering, tears running down his face, and the bag ladies are leaning over, screaming, waving their arms and hugging each other. He is a hero. He's the man who saved the joey.

He looks down at the animal in his arms. Its eyes are open, dark and shining wet, staring at his face as if it has seen God.

"Moline, one hundred forty," John Chin says aloud. He leans forward, peering down the road. "Moline, and then Iowa! Cindy, already look at all the space!" He waves his hand. "So close to Chicago."

"This is the real world," Cindy says. "Nine tenths of America is countryside."

"To think that citizens don't know this," John Chin says. He turns and looks into the backseat. "Philip, would you enjoy being a farmer?"

"I'm going to be a Baptist preacher," Philip says.

"I can't believe we're doing this," Cindy says.

"Cindy, this is important for you," John Chin says. He puts his hand gently on her shoulder. "To return to the location of a serious event in adolescence. You must be experiencing stress."

"I don't think so," she says. "What's important is going there with you."

"Are you kidnapping us?" Philip says.

"No, no," John Chin says. He smiles at Cindy. "No, your mother is taking me to see Iowa. She is driving there by choice."

"John, look," Philip says. "Guess what I am." Philip is lying stretched out on the seat, his arms at his sides, his eyes closed.

"I don't understand," John says.

"I'm a kid, napping," Philip says. "Get it? Get it, Mom?"

"Philip, that is very smart!" John Chin says. He is astonished. Cindy's son has great intelligence! To make such a joke at so young an age!

Choice, Cindy thinks. So that's it.

"I got it," Benny says. He opens his lunch sack and carefully lifts out the petri dish. "Here you go, sugar."

"Oh, Benny!" JacQuelle holds out her hands as if she's taking a holy wafer.

"It might not grow, JacQuelle," Benny says. "Johnny said we probably couldn't provide the controlled environment it needs."

"We give it love, though," JacQuelle says. She holds the dish up to the light. "Is it Asian?"

"Well, he couldn't promise on that, either," Benny says. "I figure it's like getting a kitten out of the pound. They tell you it's a female, half the time it's a tom."

"This is the beginning of the new world," JacQuelle says.

"I think we stay away from microwaves for now," Benny says. "I think we stick with the old pilot light to start out." He takes the dish and places it tenderly in the oven. "Ain't this something, baby? We been waiting a long time." He puts his arms around JacQuelle and breathes into her hair. "Now we got us something in the oven."

"Benny, you some kind of man," JacQuelle says.

Field Notes

◆

GISELLE LUNA is the world's foremost authority on the lesser flamingo. In the great tradition of experts, she lives intimately with her subjects, recording even the basest behaviors in an objective fashion. Unlike the great primate experts—Fossey, Goodall, Mead—or even other avian experts, who go so far as to mate with their subjects of study, Luna hides from hers. She moves into the blind before the flamingos come up from Africa, and stays there until they have gone back in the fall.

One day here is like another. Clouds well up and scud past, and that's about it. Everything's horizon: slick and flat, pink or gray. There's wind, occasional rain, chunks of hot air brooding over the blind, and above and under and through everything the crotcheting of flamingos, their ratchety squawks. When Luna goes inland in the fall, she hears it for weeks: the background gabbling, rising and falling like waves.

Two nights a week she meets Howell at the supply cache. They lie on the ground staring at the stars, and smoke cigarettes, and talk to each other, and all the time Giselle hears the low gabble of dozing flamingos, a carpet of bird life over the mud flats.

Giselle Luna suspects she is going to die. She has a number of reasons for suspecting this, but the one she likes best is the clarity things have acquired: her vision has sharpened, her hearing is startlingly acute. And she can smell Howell even through the smoke, even through the stink of diatom ooze rolling in on the breeze.

Five or six months a year, for twenty years, Howell has lain beside Giselle twice a week and told her his troubles. Probably she's told him hers, too, but she can only remember his stories, how he felt, what happened to him. Her stories, once told, drifted off with the tide, or dried up with the mud. She can't remember her troubles—that's another reason she thinks death is on the way.

Of course, they share their observations, too—they are collaborators. Luna trained Howell, taught him all she knew, and was pleased when he took on her specialty as his own. In the scientific press are dozens of papers giving evidence of their association, their names scrupulously alternating in precedence: LUNA, G. & HOWELL, J.G.; HOWELL, J.G. & LUNA, G. Anyone with a serious interest in flamingos knows the work of Luna and Howell.

"Tumorhead came in today," Howell says.

"She looks good," Luna says. "Flying well, too."

"A lot of extraneous neck-craning, though," Howell says. "She's gotta be blind on that side."

Even after all these years, it's only through defects and injuries that they can identify individuals. The healthy ones who can live normally are essentially identical.

"Thirty-five!" Howell says. They're counting shooting stars. One August night eight years ago they counted sixty-seven in one hour. Their record.

Giselle's eyesight is so good these days she can follow the paths of meteorites even after they cease to glow. She watches this one splash through the night sky, slow up in the atmosphere and finally drift, a dark small blob. If her eyesight had been this good forty years ago she would have been an astronomer.

Howell might have been a physician, or a cellist. He went through a phase when that was his problem: what he might have been, what he still had time to be. That was during the time he spent married. Giselle never met either wife, but she knows both daughters. Parker is a physician, and Beatrice, the younger one, plays jazz saxophone in a club in Marseilles where Giselle sometimes sings.

At last Giselle sits up. She scratches Howell's stomach as if he's a big cat and says good night. She shrugs into her load of coffee and baguettes and sets off across the mud. Even her skin knows more now. She feels creatures squirm under her feet, trying to defend themselves against her. The stars light her way onto the flats, but when she's close to the blind she knows it's there not by seeing it but because the air is different, blocked perhaps, or warmer, or cooler. She sees more than she did.

Giselle is sorry Tumorhead has come back. She's afraid she'll spend the season watching Tumorhead's behavior, hoping for clues and lessons. In fact she'll get the lesson, but she already knows what it is: Tumorhead knows nothing of her approaching death, will behave as if everything were normal, will raise another chick. And if Tumorhead could be consulted, interviewed, she'd show no interest in death. Her knowledge would begin and end with the edible things in the mud.

0430. MERCURY FADING. SMALL BREEZE SSE. ADULT MALE
FLIES, CIRCLES, LANDS IN SE QUADRANT. NO ALARM CALLS.

Luna records the date, the clouds, the time of sunrise. She pours café au lait from the Thermos and sits at the writing table, looking through the scope. In a departmental library of a large university her field notebooks are archived, hundreds of them, labeled, stored in acid-free folders, shelved chronologically. A young woman has a grant to index them, and has gotten through the first hundred or so. She showed Luna the file of index cards she's made as a preliminary catalog.

DEFECATION	MIGRATION	NESTING
DEFORMITY	MOON, PHASES OF	NIGHT
FEEDING	MORNING	NOON
MATING	MORTALITY	PREDATION

The data Luna has collected for years—one slight shift, one change of perspective, one new set of eyes, and it's a different story! It's hundreds of stories, each with a plot, a protagonist, a theme of its own. And all of them are Luna's story, the one she's been working on for so long.

"It'll all be online someday," the woman said. "Someone at Cornell wants to know the time of day flamingos feed on snails in May if there's a full moon, they pop in the keywords and they'll get it. Every entry you made, every May, under the full moon, since the start of your career. It'll all be there." She smiled. "Ideally you'd enter data directly into a file. We're working with younger scientists, with laptops, on that. Your work is the key, though. The thesaurus, the format, all derive from your work." The woman laughed and waved her arm at the room. "All this information! It's like sex, isn't it?"

> 0605. THREE JUVENILES FLY IN FROM WEST. GRAY PELI-
> CAN FLIES OVER ROOKERY, NORTH—SOUTH. ALARM HONK
> IN N. QUAD. PELICAN VEERS WEST.

Giselle hasn't seen Howell's face in . . . three years? Five? Just glimpses, a paleness in moonlight, a quick flash of the torch. But as she knows so many things now, she knows that

Howell is showing his age: his face is sinking, his forehead is lined, his eyes are loose and rimmed with blood.

"What do you do in the winter?" Howell asked the first summer.

"Go south and mate," she said. She was skinny, pale in her white cotton shorts; if her birds had seen her, they wouldn't have been alarmed.

Howell was young enough to blush; but the next winter he showed up in Arles on opening night, sitting in the back, and at four in the morning he walked her home through the walled streets to the room overlooking the Roman arena. She prefers him in the dark. There are things she chooses not to know.

She doesn't know which she'll miss more when she's dead, blind life or singing. Birds or music. She likes to think the afterlife is a jazz band, flamingos on sax, gray pelicans on percussion, little egrets coming in on the chorus. An infinite number of tables for two, red wine, plenty of floor space, and Howell, the black bulls, the white ponies, the cattle egrets, dancing through eternity, wild boars charging among them forever balancing trays loaded with little glasses of cassis. She wants it all.

A storm front moves in and passes on. Giselle Luna eats bread, cheese, and an apple. Torpor descends on the flamingos and on the blind, and Luna dozes. She's opened the roof vents, and tendrils of wind left by the storm drop in, stirring the pages of her notebooks. The sun lies heavy on the roof, its heat pressing on the flats.

What if she'd done it differently? What if she'd moved into the rookery, taken up flying, stood for hours at a time on one leg in the marsh, strolled slowly, stirring the mud, picking up an occasional small crab? Suppose she had taken an egg back to the blind. Suppose it had hatched, and she had fed a young male all year, taken it with her into town, let it sleep in her bed and sit next to the stage when she sang. And when it matured, what if she'd danced with it, sung its own song to it, let it believe they were almost—if not completely, not quite—the same creature?

But Luna has never believed in interference. This switching of eggs, this practice of casual imprinting—these are sins. This is close enough, the voyeurism she's perfected.

> 1400. SILENCE, SAVE AN INSECT, SAVE THE BUZZ OF A SMALL PLANE COMING SOUTH, PROBABLY FROM AVIGNON. PLANE CIRCLES BLIND, WRITES *LUNA* WITH ITS EXHAUST.

It's Giselle Luna's husband, Donald, who misses her.

When Giselle Luna arrived at the blind this spring, she discovered a small colony of brown bats roosting under a shutter that had slipped from its hinge. They hang motionless from before dawn until dusk, when she hears them yawning and stretching, then scritching down the wall to the edge of the shutter and jumping out into space. They're soft presences in the night, flitting over the flats, winging around the marsh. Luna can picture their squashed little faces. One hot day she unhooked one from the wall and brought it inside, gently pulled its wing wide, admiring the membrane, the long thin bones. It hardly noticed; it was in REM sleep. She put it back and its claws hooked automatically onto the rough wall of the blind.

Luna has been here for about a hundred years, and bats never roosted here before. There have been other miracles: triple rainbows, a flamingo who walked to the foot of her ladder and stood looking up at her door, remarkable birds blown out of Africa by storms, who wandered, dazed, through the flocks of flamingos, demanding and receiving *dakhala* in this alien landscape.

Howell is not a normal man. Giselle knows what he does in the winter: teaches at a university. And hs's mated at least twice. He does normal things, but his mind works differently; he doesn't interfere. His daughters grew up with little help from him, though Giselle has seen him in Beatrice's face, the way she squeezes it up when she plays, the heartiness belying the things that plague her. Still, Beatrice is not Howell, not even a reinterpretation. Howell's the story Giselle Luna reads, over and over.

His problem now is he's lost his funding. It's not surprising: money's been drying up for a decade, and finally the drought has reached even the deepest pools. But Howell's been a visiting scientist for years; he hasn't got tenure. This is his last year in the blind. Without funding, without his fieldwork, and without Luna, Howell hasn't got much.

Flamingos are primitive birds, not much more modern than their ancestors. They rarely operate outside a strict paradigm of flamingoness, which makes them an excellent study population. They have been coming to this particular rookery for more than a century; they have been feeding in the surrounding marsh since the shifting of continents created it. The notes that Giselle Luna has taken, the data that have filled a thousand notebooks, could have been recorded at any time since the world began.

The woman in the departmental library will discover a pattern. She will see that flamingo behavior does not alter from moon to moon. That the inhabitants of certain chunks of mud, carefully staked into grids and lifted out of context, vary from season to season, are cyclically abundant, and show the same alterations after passing through the digestive systems of birds and dropping into the fecund mud beneath the nests. If the woman is alert, she will find patterns in the arrival of meteors, full and partial eclipses, and the presence of land mammals inexplicably at large in the rookery. She may recognize the shapes evident in the clouds, characters from stories she herself has read—Ali Baba, Captain Hook, Madame Bovary—hovering over the rookery, peering down at the marsh, assiduously taking notes.

Giselle Luna has taken notes for half of this century. She has faithfully witnessed events, identified and selected facts, and written them down in her own language, her own notation. She herself has recorded the patterns. Now it's up to the woman in the departmental library.

> 1630. SUN AT 30°. GREAT CLOUD OF F* RETURNS TO NESTS. EVENING HONKING, EXPRESSIONS OF AFFECTION, EXHAUSTION, ANGER, BOREDOM. F* FLY IN ETERNAL FORMATION, WINGS SPREAD, LEGS AND HEADS INDISTINGUISHABLE. THEY SCREAM, SETTLE, PREEN, GROOM. THEIR VOICES DROP, THEIR TONE LOWERS TO A GABBLE. THE BACKGROUND NOISE OF DREAMS.

With darkness, Luna climbs up to the sleeping platform. She lies down on the flat roof and pulls the blankets over her. She looks up into the sky, surrounded by the clacking, the ugly murmurs of flamingos, and watches for shooting stars. She sees them everywhere. It's the one thing Howell won't believe: the number of meteors in her private sky.

In his own blind, two miles to the east, Howell's day has been nearly identical to hers. The data he records are the same. The handwriting is indistinguishable from Luna's, but by the time Luna's notebooks are indexed and the data transcribed, and his notebooks are begun, the woman on the project will have been promoted to a managerial position, and that particular pattern will remain undiscerned by the young man who follows in her footsteps.

Howell's blind is much like Luna's, though a little more cluttered and littered with pieces of eggshell. Luna's troubles are stacked carelessly on a corner of Howell's writing table, tied with old string.

When Luna dies, Howell may be the one to find her. He may walk the three miles to the supply cache, wait for her till dawn, and when she hasn't come, walk the three miles out to her blind, climb the ladder, step across the empty blind and climb the second ladder to the roof, where he will find what's left of Luna after two days in the Mediterranean sun, two cold gray rocks from space where her eyes were, pieces of her missing, already food for unknown predators.

Or he may not. She may die in Arles, keel over in the middle of a line of scat, drop at the end of a riff. She may die in a place Howell has never dreamed of.

Donald will fly out over the Mediterranean and drop the ashes into the water. He'll have given some to Howell, the ashes of her heart, perhaps, or of one thigh. Howell will carry them with him wherever it is he finds to go. He'll take a pinch of them once in a while, mixed with cassis, tucked under the cheese on a hunk of bread; swallow them, swallow Luna's heart. What else does he know?

Beatrice will play all night, her saxophone scratching through the smoke and out into the streets of Marseilles, ratcheting into the sky.

The Heaven of Animals

◆

WHEN I WAS eight years old I walked off the deck of the *Nautilus*, the world's first atomic-powered submarine, and dropped thirty feet into the harbor.

I hung there for a moment, like a cartoon dog suspended in air, before I began to fall. I could see the park at the edge of the harbor, and the people on the benches who'd been watching the waves, and the way their mouths opened into long, silent "Ohhhh!"s as I fell past.

I saw the pier at the edge of the water, and the barnacles on the black, wet pilings of the dock, and, as my feet smacked the water, I saw a Dixie cup floating on the surface.

The water was rock hard and it took my breath away. I thought I had broken my back. I kept my eyes wide open, because I always swam with my eyes open, even though my mother told me, "Taffy, you'll ruin your eyes that way." My mother thought I would ruin my eyes no matter what—reading with insufficient light, sitting too close to the television, shooting rubber bands. But try as I might, I couldn't keep my eyes closed underwater. It made me feel helpless, as if I might swim into a rock, or open them just in time to see an octopus looming up before me, about to seize me in its tentacles.

So I kept my eyes open, and I saw a school of fish gape at

me in surprise and then dart away, and I saw light green bubbles springing up around me as if I was a Fizzy. A Fizzy! I laughed out loud, and that was the only mistake I made, because I laughed out all the air I'd been holding in, and when I automatically tried to breathe, I took in water through my nose, and I thought I was going to drown.

I started to flail, and then my eyes did close, and when something grabbed me around the waist I knew it was the octopus, and I gasped in fear, and I swallowed more water, and my heart hurt, and I knew I was dead. And the octopus squeezed like crazy around my waist, and then suddenly my head popped out of the water and I took a great gulp of air and began to cry, and the octopus said, "There, there," and it was a wet sailor with white scalp showing through the bristles of his crewcut.

All around me in the water bobbed the heads of wet sailors. I couldn't stop crying, and I was furious, because the one who had grabbed me wouldn't let go.

"I can swim," I said, but talking made me cough.

"Just relax," he said, and he pulled me through the water to where another sailor knelt on the floating dock. I felt myself handed from one sailor to another, pushed from behind and pulled from above, and I rose out of the water with no effort of my own.

"I can *walk*," I said with great irritation, but the sailor lifted me like a damsel in distress and carried me up the gangplank to where my father was waiting on the pier.

"Oh, Taffy," my father said, and the sailor handed me over to him.

"Put me *down*," I said, and he did, because he was not as strong as the sailors. Someone draped a blanket over me, and my father stood there holding it around me and patting my back. Then I realized that people were cheering. I looked up; all the tourists who had been touring the *Nautilus*, and other people who were standing around on the pier, and the sailors who were climbing onto the dock, were all clapping. I had never been so embarrassed in my life.

"I turned around and you were gone!" my father was shouting at me.

"I was watching a seagull," I said, and I left it at that, because it seemed the simplest thing to do.

In fact, I had seen a different world. But later I couldn't remember it. I remembered the fall, the barnacles, the sailors. But I had bobbed to the surface too fast to get a good look at where I'd been.

It was troubling, like the words to a song just at the tip of my brain, or a memory of life before birth. I thought I'd been given a sign, some sort of evidence of another world.

I walk through the aviary on my way to work.

"Free us," whispers the Stanley Crane, sidling up to the fence. "Free us."

I stop and watch Stanley Crane, and Stanley Crane watches me, his beady gray eyes unblinking. He steps toward me, each footstep pulling his body along behind him, so that he bobs in very slow motion. "Free us," he whispers, and he hums softly, deep in his very long throat.

I look around to see who else has heard. The other birds are moving toward me, nodding, their eyes fixed on me, on my hands, their beaks curved down, moving toward the fences of their private and shared enclosures.

"Free us," they whisper and hiss. Hubbard squashes and pumpkins have grown in the pens, giant flat leaves with sudden globes shining out from beneath them.

I look at the sign on the fence. Beside his name—STANLEY CRANE—there's a blank silhouette of the African continent, with an arrow pointing from nowhere into the heart of what is probably Kenya. I close my eyes for a moment and picture acres and acres of Stanley cranes, rising in a single motion from a vast wetlands, singing out in joy and lust as they lose sight of the earth under the canopy of their own wings.

"Free us," Stanley Crane whispers, but I shake my head.

"You would be lost in the wild now," I tell him, and I step back from his cage.

He follows me to the corner of his pen as I move down the sidewalk. "Free us!" he says, and watches me walk away. "If not freedom, food!"

My mother named me after her dog. "He was the sweetest little taffy-colored cocker," my mother would say, dreamily picturing her idyllic Hoosier childhood. Then she'd look at me and frown slightly, as if she was surprised that her daughter had turned out to have brown hair.

"Ruff, ruff," I said, letting my tongue hang out and panting. "Ruff."

My mother's frown deepened. "Whatever happened to him, I wonder," she said.

I leave the aviary and go down to the building where I work, and I step inside. The building is always filled with the smell of bear, a strong, rank, ragged odor, and I breathe deep. It smells like hope to me.

This is the headquarters of the Bear Restoration Project—BRP. I've been in on it from the start—during the blue-sky days, then the planning, then the raising of funds. Now we're in the second year of implementation, and this year I am in charge of Buster and Gladly, two orphaned cubs a hunter brought us in early spring.

Last year I tried to avoid the pain of anthropomorphism by just numbering the cubs, but it didn't work. They still spoke through my friend Billings.

"HI, TAFFY," he'd say, in Ten's deep voice.

"Hey look, Taffy's here!" he squeaked in Eleven's falsetto.

This year I went back to names, and the same thing happens. "HI, TAFFY," Buster growls when I walk into the building. "Oh boy, it's Taffy!" Gladly squeaks.

Buster and Gladly have gained over eighty pounds each this summer. They pay little or no attention to the fact that I'm here: it's a good sign. They've never taken food directly from us, never been caressed by human hands. They roll around in the straw, playing silently. When one of them's in a bad mood—usually it's Gladly—they make growly, squeaky noises.

"You'd love me if I were a bear," my friend Billings has said to me, and he's probably right. "Is it my upper body under-development? Would you like it if I lifted weights?"

"Billings, you are fine the way you are," I say time and again. "I wouldn't want you any other way." And that's true too.

To tell you the truth, I'm not looking for romantic entanglements. To tell you the truth, I'm still looking for evidence of other worlds.

"More talking animals?" my brother Daniel said, grabbing my book. "'Stickytoes the Tree Toad,'" he read. "Just like you. Big flat stinky toes."

"Give it here," I said.

"Gladly," he said.

"Gladly the cross I'd bear," our mother sang, walking past in the hall.

"Listen, Taff," Daniel said. He read aloud from his own book. "'The Great Auk could be herded right across gang-planks and onto boats.'" He looked up at me. "Once, that was how life was on earth."

"Who was the Great Auk?" I said.

"They're all dead," Daniel said. "They were the original penguins, and sailors used to bash them on the head for fun."

"I don't understand you," I said. "They marched them onto their boats and bashed them on the head?"

Daniel smiled at me. "Yes," he said. "Then they ate them."

"I thought sailors were kind," I said.

"You're in outer space," Daniel said.

I listen carefully when my friends talk

ences.

"There I was, hovering a few feet above my body, watching the fireman give me the kiss of life. I didn't *want* to live," Amy says. "I floated up a long shaft of light, and at the top it was bright, and welcoming, and I knew I belonged there."

"Heaven," I say.

Amy shrugs. "I don't know," she says. "All of a sudden there was my father, at the top of this shaft of light, and I was so glad to see him. But he said, 'Go back. It's not your time.' And I thought, he's rejecting me again."

More than once my mother told me, "You're as bad as your father."

"Earth to Taffy, Earth to Taffy, come in Taffy," Daniel whined into his fist.

"Don't encourage her," said our mother.

"What's the matter with Daddy?" I said.

"His head's in the clouds," my mother said. "He's in a different world."

I pictured my father's head at the end of a very long neck, like a giraffe's neck. It drifted up there among the clouds, as he glided along the earth.

"Taffy, you'd lose your head if it wasn't tied on," said my mother. But I'd heard her say it: there was another place to be, a different world.

"I can't believe you don't know what channeling is," says my friend Lorraine. "Don't you read the papers?"

"Well, no," I have to say. "Nothing about channeling, anyway."

spirit selects someone," Lorraine says. "And then speaks
through that person. It's just a method of communicating."

"Oh, I see," I say, and I do. It's just like Buster and Gladly,
speaking through Billings.

When I was eleven years old, I was sitting one day at the
kitchen table eating a late breakfast and reading *Dr. Dolittle on
the Moon* when I happened to look idly out the window, just as
my mother, shaking the extra water out of one of Daniel's white
socks, suddenly knelt in the leaves under the clothesline, and
then lay down on the ground. I was surprised at this unex-
pected performance by my sensible mother, but not alarmed,
until a man in a bright orange vest came out of the woods a few
feet away, and stood at the edge of the yard, looking around.

I expected my mother to get up and ask the man if he
needed some help. Instead, the man walked over to where my
mother lay in the leaves. He put down his gun and knelt down
beside her, not touching her; and then, still on his knees, he
looked wildly toward the house, and right in at me.

"Call an ambulance!" he shouted, and although I couldn't
hear him through the triple-paned thermal glass, I knew what
he said.

It was the first day of hunting season.

I pay attention; and sometimes I do get hints, and messages.

"Allied horses have begun moving north," says the radio;
and I watch the south for days, looking for the clouds of dust
they'll be kicking up as they come, the Clydesdales, the
Shetlands, the pure Arabian quarterhorses.

TOADS UNDER EIGHTEEN INCHES LONG WILL BE UNDETECTED says
a sign on an overpass; and if I weren't traveling at seventy miles
per hour I'd look over my shoulder into the bed of my truck,
where hundreds of toads must be huddled together, hitching
a ride undetected, each of them under eighteen inches long.

"In winter, snowshoe hares gather in great herds," says the February page of the calendar. And sure enough, in the back-yard the snow has been trampled, flattened by hundreds of long four-toed feet, and here and there is a half-chewed carrot top, or a withered piece of iceberg lettuce.

After my mother died, Daniel and my father and I fled west, to a state where the word *wilderness* still appeared here and there on the map. As we drove across miles and miles of flat gray countryside, I dreamed of the land we were approaching: towering mountains teeming with wolves; dark, uncharted forests heavy with herds of buffalo. I'd read about the west: grizzly bears came right out on the road and looked in your car window. You could give them peanut butter, and scratch their ears.

But we moved to a city, into a house on a hill overlooking the city zoo.

"This will be nice for you, Taffy," my father said, as we stood in the backyard looking down into an enclosure where a golden eagle was perched on a log.

Someone had tied a live chicken on top of a stump for him; as we watched from our new deck, the eagle spread his one remaining wing, leaped down toward the chicken, and fell over. He scrambled around on his side in a circle, trying to stand up, the same way the chicken was scrambling around on the stump; and finally he hobbled over and began pecking at the chicken's neck.

"Oh, great," Daniel said. "A gimp eagle."

I burst into tears.

I grew up in the zoo, cleaning out cages, chopping head after head of cabbage in half, hurling unwanted Easter chicks into the pen of Walter, the one-winged eagle, and learning to watch as he tore at them until they died.

I worked my way up from cleaning cages to bottle-feeding

the newborn orangutans to handling Maizy the corn snake in the visits to schoolchildren. After I got my college degree, I went from being a volunteer to being a paid staff member; and after I got a master's degree, I became Curator of Canids.

And now I am head of the Bear Restoration Project—BRP.

My father still lives in the house overlooking the zoo. At noon I walk up the street and have lunch with him, and take him to the grocery store, the dry cleaner's, the library, wherever he needs to go.

A clot of librarians is looking out the window at the parking lot. "The poor thing," says one.

"I bet he has Alzheimer's," says another.

I catch the attention of one librarian, who comes to check my books out. "I wonder if we should do something?" the librarian says over her shoulder to her colleagues.

"And it looks like rain, too," another one says, shaking her head.

I pick up my books. "He's a physicist," I say. "He used to design submarines."

I go out to the car. "Daddy," I say, "could you try to look more purposeful?"

"What, dear?" he says, still gazing up at the clouds. "Look, cumulonimbus. We're going to get that storm after all."

This spring we cleaned out the duck pond at the zoo and dredged up everything that had accumulated there since a rich bird lover donated it half a century ago.

There was everything you'd expect: oak leaves, bird feathers, peanut shells, potato chip bags, a sneaker. Plenty of bird excrement, in various stages of decomposition. A child's doll, a plastic pinwheel that still spun when a workman blew on it, and a brassiere. An entire layer of garbage, where someone had dumped a year's accumulation: milk bottles, aluminum foil, a tea kettle with a hole in the bottom.

The deeper the workmen dug, the better preserved everything was. Comic books, with the balloons above the characters' heads still legible. A foot, later identified as that of a trumpeter swan, perfectly preserved. A nest, complete with half a dozen eggs, that looked as if it had been carefully filled with silicone and then buried in silt.

And a little girl. *She* was not perfectly preserved; only her skeleton was left. One of the workmen lifted a thick layer of black leaves and there she was, as if nothing had disturbed her for thirty years. The police thought she may have been placed there, but she could have slipped on some wet stones. She might have been watching a seagull, and stepped off the edge, and sunk to the bottom of the pond.

She sat on the mud, surrounded by eelgrass, and, looking up toward the light, she saw dozens of paddling duckfeet; as she watched, ducks plunged their heads underwater to look at the girl who was sitting in their pond. She smiled politely. Most of them looked as if they were smiling back. Small fish came out from under the overhanging banks of the pond, darting toward her shyly and quickly, ready to zip away if she reached for them. A couple of snakes wriggled through the water and slid around her, tapping against her so softly with their noses and with the sides of their ropey bodies that she thought they were kissing her.

She kept her eyes open and saw waterbugs and spiders, newts and tadpoles, and turtles, their legs waving slowly through the water. She saw the thin stick legs of a great blue heron walking slowly along near the shore, and she saw the tip of his yellow beak as he lowered his head far enough to get a glimpse of her. She saw that part of the light overhead was obscured by lilypads, and by huge black clouds of watercress, and blooms of algae on the surface.

As if she were watching a different world, she saw other girls, and their brothers, leaning over the water, and laughing, and pointing at some of the ducks who were looking down at her. There was a sudden pocking of the surface, and she knew that the people were throwing crumbs of bread into the pond for the ducks to eat.

She imagined reaching her hand up from the bottom of the pond and helping herself to a few crumbs. And at that thought she laughed, and let out the air she'd been holding for heaven knows how long, and she breathed in the dank green water of the pond and lay back in the eelgrass and looked at the light that had been the sky.

Until we dug up the girl in the pond, it had never occurred to me that worlds can be ours for the choosing.

Suppose I had stayed in the first other world I saw, down in the harbor in the shadow of the *Nautilus.* I might be there still, embedded in sand, no longer noticed by the cormorants, the harbor seals, the sea turtles who found me so startling in the beginning. I might be covered with barnacles. I could have been swallowed whole by a shark.

It might have changed everything. The sailors would have failed, my father would have looked for me in vain, Daniel would have been an only child, my mother would have had less laundry to do. I would have made it a different world for everyone.

This year I found a good place in the woods, about halfway up Raven's Hill on the west side of Mt. Umbo, under the roots of a big old spruce. I checked it out, looking out at the view to the south, lying for a while in the sun. When I decided it would do, I worked on it for days, digging the narrow entrance, then hollowing out a sleeping chamber farther in. Now it's big enough to curl up and spend the winter in. I spread dry leaves on the floor, and covered the entrance with logs and pine boughs.

Buster and Gladly have fallen asleep right on schedule. Tomorrow Billings and I and the other members of the Bear

Restoration Project—BRP—will sedate them, pull them out of their pen, and fit them with radio collars. Then we'll load the sleeping bears into a big wooden crate and set off for Mt. Umbo.

Mt. Umbo is covered with snow. We'll drive in as far as we can in the Wildlife Service truck, and then we'll pull the bears out of their crate and stuff them into heavy canvas sacks. We'll have to go the rest of the way on snowshoes—four people, hauling bags full of bear. It will take a couple of hours to reach the den that I dug out last summer, and that we cleared the snow away from last week.

We'll empty Buster and Gladly out of the bags, check one last time for regular heartbeats and steady breathing, and then stuff them into the den, along with the straw they've been sleeping in. This is the hardest part: scratching their stubby ears for the last and only time, sniffing their bear odor, saying good-bye.

Then we'll pull the pine boughs back over the entrance, and shovel on a load of snow for insulation, and head back down the hill.

I'm not fooling myself that I'm helping to save the world, or the animal kingdom, or even a certain species of black bear. The project really has nothing to do with all that. It's only Buster and Gladly I'm thinking of.

Sometimes I dream of the *Nautilus*, of climbing out through the hatch and stepping off the deck into nothing. I relive every second and inch of that fall into cold green water. I go through it all in the dream, up to the second that the octopus grabs me and I struggle in vain toward the surface. I wake up with a start, gasping for air.

To calm myself, I close my eyes again, to see it as my mother might have seen it from the shore.

"There went Daddy," she would say, "stumbling along with his head in the clouds. And there came you, right behind him, just the same way. But you kept going straight, and you dropped right over the edge, and my heart stopped."

Here my mother's eyes would open wide with remembered horror, and she would reach out to touch my hair. "But before you even hit the water, every sailor on the deck of the *Nautilus* had jumped overboard. And it looked like a storm of pure white birds, or angels, falling into the sea to save your life."

I like to believe my mother got into the heaven of animals by mistake.

"Taffy's mother? That's not the information I was given," St. Peter says, frowning down at his list. "It says here 'White-tail deer, eight-point buck, first day of hunting season.'"

"Oh, no," my mother says. "That was me, hanging out laundry. It was just Daniel's sock."

St. Peter shakes his head. "Sorry, but the rules are the rules."

My mother turns away; and, neatly sidestepping my father's head, she bounds across the clouds, and trots up the gangplank to the other gate.

"We've been waiting!" says a Great Auk. "But where are your antlers?"

"I guess I'm a doe," my mother says.

The Great Auk shakes his head. "Mistakes have been made," he says, and a sailor with great white wings opens the gate, and my mother goes in.

The last I see of her, she's walking slowly through the clouds, holding her head low, and a golden-haired cocker spaniel, who has been waiting for a long time, leaps about, yipping happily, nipping at her ears.

It's the heaven I'll choose, if I get the chance.

With luck, Buster and Gladly will sleep till spring. When they wake up, they won't be scared, because they'll have each other, and they'll have the same old straw they went to sleep with, smelling of bear, mostly, but with just a hint of their old friend Taffy. They'll snorkel around, stretching, yawning, and then push their way out of the den into a different world.

Of course, it's not really a different world. It's their old world, the one they belong in; it's just that now they'll be here without their mother. And after a while, they'll separate, probably without so much as a farewell. Buster will be on his hind feet somewhere, reaching for some berries, and Gladly will wander off over the top of the hill; and that will be that. They'll be alone.

And that, of course, is how they would have ended up anyway.

Flatus Vocis

◆

FLATUS VOCIS: a mere name, word, or sound without a cor-
responding objective reality
           —*Webster's Third New International Dictionary*

The summer is so hot there is a spontaneous human com-
bustion on the south side. Purée is working triage in the
ER when they bring her—it had been a woman—in. "Just
molten flesh," Purée says. "Molten flesh and a beating heart."

Purée works long days, and if my light is on when she gets
home she comes upstairs, stripping off her greens as she
comes. Barry comes up from his air-conditioned apartment,
and we sit in the kitchen in our underwear drinking gin and
playing cards, smoking dope and staring out at the red lights
blinking on top of the John Hancock building. Purée has
been up so long she can't sleep, and she tells us ER tales.
She loves working ER. "Never a dull mo," she says.

Barry is half in love with her, despite her sex, and he gets
so engrossed in her stories, the glow of her black skin through
the lace of her underwear, that he loses every hand. I laugh
at him and kick him under the table as he stares at her smoky
hair, her pearly nails, but I'm in love with her too. She's like
a person from another universe, living in the second-floor

apartment like sandwich filling between us. Her father was
Maasai but she was born in St. Paul in February, and when
dawn starts spilling out of the lake and the two of them go
downstairs, I lie in my sweaty sheets dreaming of Purée in
her lace in the snow, thinking of how the ice-encrusted snow
would feel against her back if it were mine, seeing face cards
turning over and over before her, until Beep thrusts his nose
into my neck, demanding a walk.

When we go downstairs Beep rushes ahead as far as Purée's
door, where he stands with his head cocked, ears up, nose
shoved against the latch. He snuffs loudly, snorts, snuffs
again and listens.

Inside on his perch, Flatus hears the snuffing and screams.
"Son of a bitch!" he yells, accurately. "Son of a bitch! Yo
mama! Eat shit, mothafucka!"

Beep growls and starts to dance about on stiff legs. I grab
him before he can launch into his deep-throated barking and
haul him downstairs. It's an indication I want to control
things, I suppose. Why not let him bark, indulge his dogly
nature, converse with Flatus through the door?

Beep and I walk the alleys, grateful for the darkness we
pretend is cooler than daylight. The air drips with moisture
but the spaces between streetlights are black.

I suppose I have a sort of death wish, out in the alleys at
night, but it's a good neighborhood, a blue-collar neighborhood where hausfraus still scrub their steps every morning,
where the gang graffiti is whitewashed by ten A.M. There are
plenty of cops around; it's a strong Democratic ward, until
only recently pure white.

I do not socialize much, but I have my acquaintances. Most
nights I turn a corner and there's John with his hands in his
pockets, whistling as he strolls down the alley. Rick's trotting
back and forth, checking out who's been pissing there, and
he rushes up to stick his nose into my crotch and inhale, then

takes off with Beep. They flash from streetlight to streetlight, sniffing like mad.

"Nice night," John says.

I reluctantly shook John's hand the night he introduced himself and Rick, but there's a strict alley etiquette, and I don't take his arm as we walk. In the alley you do not touch people.

"Smoke?" John says, and I take a drag, the sweet cloud filling my lungs and drifting around my head. We walk slowly, passing the joint back and forth, watching Beep and Rick. "God!" John shouts, stretching his arms overhead. Rick races out of the darkness and laughs up at him, then disappears again. "Twenty-hour day!" John says. He works construction. "Onsite since four. I want to retire now!"

I look at John's face under the streetlight; he's older than I'd thought but not more than fifty, not old. "What would you do?" I say.

"Lord, what wouldn't I do?" he says. "Take Rick to the country. Visit my wife in Santa Fe. Oh, lord, I'd dance." And right there in the alley he puts his arms around some woman I can't see and bends her over backwards, then pulls her up and takes off, twirling her down the alley in perfect time. Rick flies after, and Beep comes back to me. "Good night!" John calls, and he dances around the corner.

When Purée is on call and stays at the hospital overnight, I leave Beep upstairs and go down to feed Flatus. Flatus lives in the bedroom, where he spends most of his time trying to peel the frame away from the window. I think he's trying to escape, but Purée says he just likes the exercise. She keeps the window closed, though; Flatus could rip through the screen in seconds.

Flatus is perched on the windowsill when I open the bedroom door. "I'm ready, baby," he whispers, rocking back and forth. "Give it to me." When I hand him a kibble he makes a sound like a sneeze before he accepts it in his snaky claw, and he turns it over and over, checking its authenticity, as I fill his water dish and pour more pellets into his food tray. Though Purée has never asked me to, I clean up the floor, which is spotted with large, gelatinous chunks of parrot guano. Flatus watches from one sarcastic eye, his head on one side, and chuckles from time to time.

Flatus spends a lot of time alone. Once when I go in, he is standing at the window stretching his neck excitedly, cooing at the pigeons that live under Lucky Lazarro's eaves next door. Flatus has it down: the rootling, the rustling of feathers, the scratching of toes on asbestos shingles.

"Evisceration," Purée says. "On a flight from L.A. to O'Hare. This fat lady flushes a toilet while she's still sitting on it, and the suction disembowels her."

Purée's eyelashes curl up, and her trout-shaped eyes tilt. Her eyes are such that you could suspect her of deceiving you with her stories, of mocking your credulity, of despising you for your color or your sex, of ridiculing your devotion, your inferior education. Purée's eyes are so beautiful, she would be easy to disbelieve. But I don't.

Once when I am watering the tomatoes, Lucky Lazarro comes out from behind his roses and leans over the fence. The sun bounces off his head and I keep my sunglasses on. "That doctor," he says. "She's a tough customer, ain't she?"

I have to admit that I was afraid of her for a long time. She is over six feet tall, she moves like a cheetah, and she is one of many people I would not like to meet in a dark alley. But I love her now. "Purée?" I say, and laugh.

Lucky nods. His eyes are tiny slits.

When it gets late, twelve or one or two, Barry comes upstairs and we wait for Purée. We have strict rules and limits: we never learn her schedule. Sometimes she comes and sometimes she doesn't.

Barry was wounded in love in the spring, and it's all he thinks about. "I found a dead dog on the beach once," he says. "Its eyes were gone, it was swollen and it had no feet."

I glance at Beep, who's twitching in his sleep. "I watched them pull a child out of the lagoon last winter," I say. "He was in a coma for weeks, but he was brain-dead."

Barry's a sensitive man. He can't listen to the lyrics of any song, or pick up a golf ball—his lover was the pro at a club in Winnetka—without welling up. He had planned to be an artist, but it fell through, and now he's housesitting for his Uncle Leon, my landlord, who is on a Guggenheim, dating fossil primate skulls with an electron microscope in the Far East. He does not know what to do next. "I was there when they brought some bodies out of a burning house," he says. "In plastic bags."

I can do better than that. I remember a Buddhist monk immolating himself on the steps of the state capitol.

We are not obsessed with Purée; it is not like that; but when she finally comes running up the stairs, tossing her clothes over the bannister, we hold our breath, our faces turned toward the door, till she enters the kitchen. Beep thumps the floor with his tail, and Purée slides into her chair.

"Babies," she says. "Ten years old, and nobody noticed she's the size of a hubbard squash. 'We run to fat,' her mama says." Purée leans back laughing, her neck stretched tight and every cord vibrating.

In the alley a turtle is making his way toward Damen Avenue and certain death. Beep sniffs at it, but the turtle does not flutter; it shows no sign of fear. It keeps plodding. I poke at it with a stick and succeed in turning it toward an overgrown yard, but after a few steps it pivots on one leg and heads for the street again.

"Stubborn, ain't he." A man has been watching from behind a hedge.

"Should I take him to the lagoon?" I say.

"Rats'll get him." The man comes out of his yard and I see that he has a hook for one hand. He picks the turtle up and its legs wave foolishly in the air. It does not even pull its head into the shell. "I'll take care of it," the man says.

There is nothing I can do. "Thanks," I say, and I walk away fast. Tears run down my face. Somehow, and I do not know how, I know the hook-handed guy is going to eat the turtle.

Near home, a cop car creeps along the alley after us until we're under a streetlight, then accelerates and pulls up even with us. It is two A.M. and the cop rolls down his window and takes off his shades. "Seen any Ricans?" he says.

"Any what?" I say, before I can think.

"Puerto Ricans," he says, his voice drawn back in his throat. His nametag says SCHNOOR.

"No," I say, and he rolls the window up, and the car slides silently away. I follow Beep out of the alley and around the corner past the Shady Nook Tavern, thinking, Schnoor?

Purée tells us about her dates. She does have dates, but as far as I know she is not involved in affectionate relationships. She goes out with men she could not possibly like. Maybe they give money to the hospital. Maybe they are hospital administrators.

She goes out with an obese man, and there is nothing jolly about his obesity. It is more like an insult. He takes Purée to a ritzy restaurant and he chooses food you do not want to watch a fat man eat. Purée can hardly stand to watch him eat it, the drumsticks of birds, grease dripping into his beard, terrible sounds when he crunches on bones and tendons. He makes good conversation, he talks brilliantly about literature and economics, he knows the politics behind the recent reorganization of the hospital managerial staff. Every time Purée picks up her glass of wine he stops chewing, fork halfway to his mouth, and watches her throat as she swallows; then he goes back to his food.

He takes her to his condo. They go up in an elevator to the thirty-ninth floor and step into his living room, which is bigger than Purée's apartment. He takes her over to the window. "Years ago," he says, "when I was a young man, I stood looking out at the city and said, 'Someday all this will be mine.'"

Purée is disappointed by the evening. "I don't make many demands," she tells us over cards. "There isn't much I want. I was hoping for some affection, but all he did was drool on me."

"Among the Maasai," Purée says, "female circumcision is still common. They use sharp, not particularly clean knives, and no anesthetics, no antibiotics. The clitoris and the external labia are removed. And if you think these things don't go on here, you living on the moon." She lays down three queens and a run of spades. "Gin."

Sometimes Beep and I come in the back way, and we stand in the yard looking up at her window. She keeps the lights on all night, and she talks to Flatus in her cool rolling voice, and he replies. Their voices are identical, and I can't figure out who is saying what to whom.

"I ain't my brother's keeper," someone says in Purée's voice.

Officer Schnoor takes Purée out to dinner. Barry and I do not really wait up for her, but we are playing gin rummy on the floor in front of the fan when she comes in. She runs past her own door and by the time she steps over the fan, her shirt is off.

"My first ride in a Jaguar," she says, and pours herself some gin. "We drive around smoking some weed and drinking whiskey out of a paper cup, looking at the outsides of health clubs he's invested in. Then we go to Trader Vic's. I got one of those candy drinks with a little toy whore in it." She shows us her souvenir.

"So," Barry says. "Have a good time?"

"I got me a headache," Purée says. "I had to come home

early." She grins, and I grin, and I see that Barry's a grinning fool.

"What a day," Purée says. "They bring in this four-year-old child. Her eyes are open, she's breathing, but her skin is flaking off and her little arms and her little legs are as hard as stone. Her mama and daddy have baked her in an oven. They put her in at four hundred degrees to bake the Devil out of her. I brought us something." She takes a tape out of her bag and goes and puts it on my tapedeck. Strange, uneven rhythms start lumping out of the speakers. At first I think there's something wrong with the tape, but then Purée lies down on the other side of Barry and pushes her shoes off with her toes. "Know what that is?" she says. "Heart sounds. Murmur, arrhythmia, fibrillation, flutter, tachycardia. Aneurysmal bruit."

I reach up and turn out the light, and we lie listening to dozens of human hearts. There's a little beep that signals the start of each new one; without it I wouldn't be able to tell when one ends and the next begins.

"It takes a lot of practice," Purée says. "It takes years to tell these hearts apart."

It would be so much easier if I could be in love with Barry, and he with me. Sometimes he lies on a chaise in the backyard, smeared with oil, wearing nothing but a lime green bikini. I stare down at him from my back porch; it's almost the only time he leaves the house. He even orders his groceries by phone and has them delivered. I can see Lucky Lazarro staring at him from behind his rose bushes.

I worry about Barry, but Purée says he'll be all right. She says she sees it all the time. "Broken hearts always streaming into the ER," she says. "You reach a certain age and condition, your heart can only take so much. Bang! Infarct."

I am not attracted to Barry. He is too thin.

Or if I could really be in love with Purée. I could be her

wife, keep house for her, wash and iron her blue cotton scrubs, whip up a lunch of yogurt and banana and brewer's yeast and pour it in her Thermos, lie reading every night till she gets home. I would feed Flatus and clean up around his perch. Beep would be kind to Flatus, and Flatus would not persecute Beep.

Purée sleeps on a wrestling mat spread on the living room floor. She uses no pillow. I imagine her there underneath me, lying flat on her back staring at the ceiling. I lie on my stomach mashing my face into the mattress which, though it is extra firm, is probably too soft for Purée. I mash my face down and imagine it directly over hers. Only layers of wood, cotton, and air separate us.

"This guy is walking down the stairs," Purée says. "He's carrying his hairbrush, and he trips. He falls down the stairs and lands face down on the floor, jamming the bristles into his eyeballs."

Lucky Lazarro is at the door. It's unheard of, Lucky coming to our door. Mostly the neighbors leave us alone. Me they tolerate because I water the tomatoes and I wear glasses. Barry they avoid. Purée? They watch her from behind their venetian blinds and they don't know how to think about her.

"That doctor," Lucky says. "Is she here?"

"Purée!" I call, and she comes to her door in her underwear and looks down.

Lucky stares at her, trying to see her nipples through the lace. "We got a problem," he says. "I don't like to call the cops. But I think Chet Pinkowski is sick."

"What are the symptoms?" Purée says.

"He don't answer his door," Lucky says. "He always answers his door but now he don't."

We follow Lucky Lazarro down the alley and into a back-yard I have passed many times. The graffiti on the garage has not been painted over in weeks. Lucky knocks on the door, and when there is no response he pushes it open.

Inside it smells like catfood and sulphur. Lucky pulls a chain in the ceiling and a light goes on, and we are in a kitchen filled with newspapers. Newspapers are stacked to the ceiling, in orderly piles, six deep from the walls. It is very cleverly arranged, some of the newspaper stacks the height of a kitchen counter, and on one is a dish of catfood and an old bologna sandwich. There is a corridor through the newspapers, and Lucky leads us through. "I never came inside before," he says. "Holy mother of God."

We march into a hall that is also lined with stacks of newspapers. We turn a corner and the sulphur smell whacks us in the face like a sound barrier. "We got trouble," says Purée.

Lucky pushes open a door that is the door to Chet Pinkowski's bedroom. I realize I have seen him before: he is the hook-handed guy. Now he is putrefying on his narrow bed, and on the bedside stack of newspapers is a birdcage full of dead canaries.

"Holy shit," Lucky says. Barry makes a choking sound behind me.

Purée walks over and picks up Chet Pinkowski's loose arm. "He is long gone," she says. She actually looks at his eyeball. She looks at Lucky. "Friend of yours?"

Lucky, most of his face covered with handkerchief, shakes his head. "No," he says. "My newspapers were piling up."

We wait in the front yard for the police. Officer Schnoor pulls up in his car. He takes off his shades and says something into a walkie-talkie. He comes into the yard. He takes all our names. He pretends he does not know Purée, but he stares at me. "Do I know you?" he says.

"No," I say.

"Okay," Purée says. "They bring this middle-aged white male in, a little portly. He's in his bathrobe, and his urethra is hanging half out of his penis, and his testicles are swollen the size of footballs. 'What happened?' I say. 'I don't know,' he says. 'I was vacuuming the stairs, and the next thing I knew the thing was sucking me off.' "

"What about the good things?" Barry says. "What about the caring, the love that goes on in the ER?"

"I don't tell you the bad things," Purée says. "I don't talk about the really bad things."

What are we to believe? It's all true. What happens to Purée down there, what does she think? How did she learn to cope with junkies, sadists, people with running sores? Did she always sleep on a wrestling mat? She's got black-as-midnight skin but she was raised to value truth and beauty.

What would happen to me? That's why I watch Purée.

The summer is so hot there are municipal brownouts. We check the paper for scheduled brownouts in our area. In some sections of town there are none, but in our good safe neighborhood they happen often.

During the brownouts I walk in the alley with John and Rick and pretend I'm in the country. There are crickets in uncut lawns and under hedges, and I can see a few stars. I squint at them, listening to Beep's steam-engine breathing as he keeps his nose to the ground.

John thinks I am scared by what happened to Chet Pinkowski. He's right, but I'm not as scared by the way he died as by how he lived. For all I know he was happy, but I don't want to be obsessed.

I have a recurring dream. I am pushing a grocery cart through an endless alley in the snow. I am a specialist in cans, and I stop at every garbage bin, filling my cart with cans. Every night as I'm about to reach the end of the alley Beep picks up a can and turns to look at me. "No!" I shout, just as his teeth puncture the can. It is full of lye. Lye fills his mouth and pours down his throat. I wake myself up, and Beep is staring at me in my bed.

"John," I say, "why do you stay here?"

"I don't want to die," he says.

Purée was the Iowa State High School Girls' Wrestling Champion for three years running. It is hard to imagine Purée living among soybeans. It is hard to imagine her wrestling Iowa farm girls, too, wrapping her black limbs around their corn-fed bellies, flinging her viny arms around their pulsing brutish necks in standard takedowns, leaning into their shoulders and pinning them. Whispering, telling them stories, threatening them softly, her voice so low they don't know for sure that they hear it, just a whisper, a breath, a flutter of their own hearts. They always cry; it is the way girls express frustration; but by the time the coaches and the parents see that it is a pattern, Purée is long gone.

Maybe that is how Purée became accustomed to touching strange skins. Why she doesn't mind a little alien sweat. The thought of touching strangers, feeling for nodes in their armpits, checking strange women's vaginas for lesions, even wrapping tissue-soft upper arms with Velcro and listening to how the blood flows up, then down, is enough to turn me pale and sickish. But Purée was a champion of rolling in the sweat of teenaged girls.

Once when I look down into the yard, Barry is lying on his back on the chaise in a fuchsia-colored bikini. His eyes are closed and he is listening through a stethoscope to the sounds of his own heart.

He is all sinew, all cartilage and bone. He lies perfectly still, one hand holding the bell of the stethoscope against his chest. I imagine what he hears: the rush of air when he breathes, the sigh of blood oozing through his veins. He moves the stethoscope into his armpit and closes his arm over it.

I have lived here for a long time. Purée moved in the week after I did—no moving van, no husky men swearing at the narrow staircase, just her wrestling mat and Flatus. Barry has been here since Uncle Leon left for the Far East.

"Who do you love?" I say to Beep, who stands beside me.

His nostrils quiver, taking in the smells: Lucky Lazarro's roses, the insecticide he doses them with, the rotting garbage in the cans behind the garage, Barry's coconut oil suntan lotion, the dogshit in the alley, the beef grease being vented from the Shady Nook, my sweat, the fresh-cut grass. These are just a few of the things Beep smells, but he loses interest. He does not answer my question but backs away from the window until he can turn around, and he goes to lie down in front of the fan.

Down in the yard, Barry shakes his head without opening his eyes.

Beep wakes up after a long sleep on the kitchen floor. He is alone: I have not come back from wherever I've gone without him. He stretches; he lifts his head, bites an itchy spot on his right front paw, then stares into space, listening for anything. He hears Flatus cooing downstairs, but now is not the time to care.

Beep yawns and heaves himself to his feet. He walks into the bathroom and has a long drink from the toilet. He walks back into the kitchen and starts to lie down in front of the door, where he was before, but he stops. He hears a fly.

If there is anything that infuriates Beep, it's a fly. He hates the way they buzz incessantly and settle on the tips of his ears when he's asleep or try to drink the moisture from his nose. They are despicable things; he kills them at every opportunity. He is very good at catching and dispatching them.

Beep trots into the living room, ears up. He locates the fly; it is behind the gauzy white curtain, buzzing against the upper half of the window. The window's open; in fact it is wide open, because I took the screen out when I shook the mop out the window this morning, and I forgot to put it back in. Beep does not notice the screen standing against the wall beside the window. His attention is fixed on the irritating fly buzzing behind the gauze.

Beep gets close, ears up, eyes on the fly. The fly is almost within reach; the window is at floor level. I have to bend over to look through it, to watch the buses pass along the street below, but it is just the right height for Beep. Late in the afternoon on days when I go to work, Beep rouses himself from his daylong sleep and stations himself at the window, and he watches the cars, the bicycles and dogs, the cat on the porch across the street, the taxis and motorcycles and trucks. He sees every movement below as he waits to catch sight of me coming home.

At the moment he's only interested in the damned fly. The buzzing infuriates him. He stretches out his neck, sniffs. The fly buzzes. Beep lunges.

The gauze curtain is like a slight bit of cool cloud, a slippery breath, as he falls against it and out the window. Beep is not an athletic dog; he does not twist in the air, and his legs do not flail as he hovers for a comical split second above the sidewalk. He is a big lumpy dog and he falls heavily, one instant maddened by a fly, the next instant all of Damen Avenue rushing up at him. He hits the roof of the porch and scrabbles there for a second, but he slips and goes on falling, another fourteen feet, and lands with a thud on the tiny patch of lawn that Barry has trouble remembering to mow.

Barry is in the basement looking at the assortment of tools on Uncle Leon's workbench. In his stint as a sculptor, and during the time when he tried to make interesting art out of pieces of wood and cockatiel feathers, Barry learned how to use certain tools: a hammer, a staple gun, a soldering iron. But he doesn't know how to use most of Uncle Leon's equipment, and in fact he doesn't know what most of it is.

He is standing in front of the workbench when he hears a sudden soft whump, and he looks out the window just above his head and sees the face of Beep in front of him, Beep's head resting in the grass, his nose an inch from the window, his stomach two inches from the white picket fence.

Barry tells me this as I sit on the floor of his apartment with tears running down my face. I am stroking Beep's head, cradling him in the pink blanket Lucky Lazarro put over him when they carried him inside. Barry waited beside the door for hours, to catch me before I could go upstairs and find the empty apartment, the open window.

The summer has been hotter than any living being can remember, but now the weather breaks, and the temperature drops to the seventies at night. When Barry knocks on my door, I do not answer. Beep, lying beside me on the mattress I have dragged into the living room, growls softly, but of course he does not get up. I know Barry is standing outside the door, listening to the sound of my television, but I don't move, and before long he goes away.

Beep and I don't care what's on TV. It's a waste of energy, we feel, to change channels, so we watch whatever comes on next. Tonight we are watching the finals of the International Ballroom Dancing Competition. I am inexpressibly disappointed: the women wear ridiculous fluorescent costumes that expose their private parts, and the men have pimples. But suddenly, as the finalists break into a tango, the camera zooms in on a man in a skintight pink tuxedo. For a moment I can't place him, without Rick beside him; but then he grins, and as I see the flash of gold in his molars I realize John has made it to the finals.

The street door opens downstairs; I hear Barry come out of his apartment, and I hear Purée's cool laugh. Then Purée's footsteps come upstairs, but they stop on the second floor and she goes into her own apartment.

Late that night Beep and I inch our way down, me going in front as he drags his hindquarters from step to step.

Barry's door is open just a crack. "I don't think I want to know," he's saying, as Beep hits the bottom step.

"You got to," Purée says. "I know the lab techs. Nobody knows the results but you and me. Come on, boy," she says. "Make a fist."

Outside, and down the last seven steps, Beep and I rest. The street is quiet; it is very late. When Beep's panting slows to normal breathing I pass the towel under his belly and hold the ends up, so that his back half is caught in a sling. We walk slowly to the end of the block and into the alley, where I take the sling off and Beep crawls from hedge to fence to utility pole, sniffing out the spots he needs to mark.

We do not go far. I catch him up in the towel again and we make our way back to the front steps. Beep sniffs at the picket fence, then drops his head and stares at the lowest step. He sighs.

The truth is, I don't want to love Purée, I don't want to be her wife. I want to wear her thick rich skin, carry her eyelids over my own eyes, throw my arms around the neck of a junkie who's thrusting his knife into the skin of an ER orderly's scrotum.

I want to explode, my noxious gases finally bursting out of the prison of my own pale skin. I want Purée to scrape me up off the sidewalk and cry over me. I do not want to love Purée.

I will take Beep to live on an island. He will lie in the sun watching chipmunks, raccoons, jays; and at night we will hear the screams of porcupines and the singing of coyotes on the far side of the pond. He will die a sudden, painless death in my arms at the age of 101 in dog years, and leave me free to love again.

Purée has left the bedroom door open, and Flatus wastes no time in going through it. He swaggers across the floor and steps onto the wrestling mat. It's got a strange smooth texture; he slips, and angrily he pokes a hole in it with his claw; seizing one edge in his beak, he backs away, listening with great pleasure to the ripping sound it makes. He drops it and imitates the ripping sound exactly.

He leaves a turd on the wrestling mat and jumps up to the

windowsill. It is a different view here: not the pigeons under Lucky Lazarro's eaves but a wide bright street lined with trees, and it stretches as far as Flatus can see. He cranes his neck, turning his head to look in the other direction, and the street is endless that way too. Flatus's heart beats rapidly.

It's easy to gouge a hole in the screen, and to rip the screen to shreds.

There is a universe of birds out there. In the darkness there are swallows, and owls, and birdlike bats; and in the morning there will be hundreds of pigeons, whose language Flatus already speaks, and robins, and gulls, and sparrows. And beyond the streets and houses is the park, where flocks of escaped parrots live in the trees and feed on grasshoppers and leftover fries. In the winter they huddle together for warmth on the arc lights above Lake Shore Drive, and many of them die; but it is summer now.

Flatus steps through the torn screen and stands on the ledge, the noise of the city rushing up to him. He chuckles, and screams. He jumps into the air, and flaps his wings, and he is flying. He has never flown so high or so well. "Up yours, mothafucka!" he screams. He makes the perfect sound of a human heart gone awry, and beeps, and flies east, toward the lake, where the free parrots roost in the trees.

My Life in the Frozen North

◆

I WAS the child of explorers.

My mother dropped me inside a little hut made of ice when the temperature outside was sixty-five degrees below zero, Fahrenheit. If my father hadn't, just the day before, waited for nineteen hours beside a hole in the ice for a seal to put its nose out of the water to breathe, and shot it in the face, instantly grabbing its flailing form and yelling bloody murder until my mother, already in labor, waddled out of the hut to grab the seal's flipper and help my father ease the thing into the world on this side of the ice—well, they might have been hungry enough to take a look at me, red and steaming and looking as much like a seal's guts as anything else they ever saw, and carve out my tiny liver and heart for a treat, and try out my layers of babyfat to keep their lamp burning for another week.

But full of blubber and fresh blood as they were, they instead delighted in touching my slimy limbs; and my thin wails were music to my mother's ears, my father being almost totally deaf after years of shooting seals and polar bears without adequate ear protection.

"I shall call her Floe," my mother said.

My father was from central Indiana, and my mother was

from Medicine Hat, but they left those homes as soon as they reached their majorities and headed north. They met en route and were never parted. On reaching the north they at once settled into the life that was available to them, namely subsistence living among what remained of the native population. In this way they learned to live *of* and *with* the country, rather than against or in spite of it, and so survived numerous mishaps that might have stopped less intrepid newcomers to the region.

It is not my purpose to detail their early struggles here; this is not their story, but mine.

My parents had never thought of offspring.

"How innocent I was!" my mother would often sigh as we sat around inside whatever igloo we'd built to pass the winter season, which, in most of the places we lived when I was growing up, lasted from August to early July. "I thought procreation was a matter of choice!"

My father, if he was present, would laugh his great, booming laugh, one that shook the very ice cubes in the walls. "Foolish child!" he would say fondly to my mother, stroking her few remaining hairs. Then they would send me outside to play with the dogs while they discussed adult matters.

As soon as I could be apart from my mother for a few hours at a time, my father began taking me with him on his hunting expeditions. We would head out onto the ice, where my father chopped a hole that he thought would look inviting to a seal desperate for oxygen. Then he would wrap himself in a sheet and put me, mewling and puking as I was, in a little pile at the edge of that hole, as encouragement; his reasoning being, no doubt, that a seal would never believe it possible that a compassionate human man could use his own helpless infant child as bait. Thus, seals never hesitated to breathe near where I lay. My father was a great hunter, and bagged many seals. I grew up loving the aroma of hot fat and raw flesh, and my garments were made of the strong, sparsely haired hide of seals.

The law of life in the Frozen North is Eat. Sometimes we ate our dogs, who would have eaten us if we had ceased our vigilance. Once a ship full of jolly Germans landed and seized our dogs while my parents lay disguised under a sheet, quivering with fear, which happened to make them look like a piece of the natural landscape because it was nearly summer and the ice was in constant flux. They had left me beside a seal's breathing hole in their rush to safety, but the Germans never harmed or even touched me, for despite my parents' fears, they weren't cannibals, but merely Europeans.

My parents were explorers, not Christians. Their religion was the northward journey, the discovery of nameless seas, the measurement of the immeasurable depths of ice in the north polar region. Ever restless, ever searching for an ice-free passage, they never stayed on one floe for more than a winter but moved on at the first sign of breakup in July. Many a time, tiny as I was, I hopped from floe to floe in the path of my parents, who couldn't carry me because they were carrying great loads of raw meat and guns.

Of course, nothing remained of the world to be discovered, it being already the second half of the twentieth century, A.D. This never stopped my parents, though; forever searching, they paid no attention to the disinterest of society in them and their discoveries. They wandered, checking latitudes, altitudes, and the thickness of the ice, recording all in great notebooks with waterproof pages. When a notebook was filled to capacity with these records, they wrapped it in indestructible plastic and buried it in the permafrost.

"For posterity," my mother would say.

"You little dickens!" my father chuckled every time.

From time to time I find one of these notebooks. What a strange feeling it is to discover messages in my own parents' hands, messages not to *me* but to others whom I've never met or heard of! "80° 16'," one message might read; and what long, winding trails of memory such figures send me off on! I can hear my father's voice even now, when he's been dead and frozen for more years than he was alive, calling out the readings from his theodolite; I can see my mother squatting on the ice, her frigid fingers shaking with the cold as she struggled to record accurately the numbers he shouted. The numbers are all I have of them now, for after an early accident in which my mother was struck a glancing blow on the head by an enraged polar bear sow whose offspring my father had thoughtlessly carved up right on the ice, my mother was never able to read or write words; she suffered from a form of alexia that left only her ability to recognize numerals intact.

My father disdained to write at all, and so except for these rows and rows of digits there is no written record of their times and discoveries; and I myself, though able to recognize them as numbers, was never taught to use them, so they mean nothing to me.

Why would a man and woman choose such a life? I have often pondered this question, for I have had little else to do since my parents died. I am greatly skilled at survival. I spend all my time alone, and only bother to speak now because I share the human desire for immortality. I think I can have some effect on what the world does with and to itself; I think it can take a lesson from me. The lesson it will take, of course, is the truth that a single life makes no difference in even the medium run; the individual life means nothing more than does the collective life, which is nothing. Still, we try to make a difference; it is our greatest failing.

I remember my mother chewing endlessly on the skin of seals, softening it to slice into leggings for my spindly little legs. Her teeth dropped out before she reached her thirtieth year. No hair, no teeth; and yet she loved me, in her way.

My father, having grown up in the hog capital of the world, loved the dogs as he had loved the hogs of his youth, as pets and as meat; and I myself have never known a more delightful treat than fresh-killed newborn pup. As a little child I danced with eagerness for the tiny, still-pulsing heart; usually it went to my father, a voracious eater, but now and then it dropped to the ice and I scrambled after it, screaming shrilly. My father laughed to watch. "Like my own youth in the mud," he'd say, and continue chortling softly as he took the puppy livers and the tiny intestines, soft and empty, a great delicacy to an icebound man.

Dogs were companions, too. And slaves.

"Floe," my mother said more than once, "a man is nothing without a dog." This rang true for me; as I watched my father hunt, sitting for hours beside a hole in the ice, poised to shoot a seal in the face, I saw that he was indeed nothing.

But when he ran along behind his dogs, shouting and whipping them, and their whines rang out across the ice, I saw his strength.

Music! Of this I know nothing, for my parents never sang.

We lived atop the world, waiting for one season to pass so that we might live through another. Playmates I had none, save the ever-hungry dogs. They were massive, snarling brutes, with crazed white eyes that watched unblinking as I hopped across the little crevices that were my playground. The worst were chained, and I have no doubt they were unable in their dogly minds to distinguish between me and, say, a fat baby seal, or a little playful fox kit—any of us would make a tasty snack for a dog in the North.

My father fed the dogs once every three or four days. "A hungry dog is keen!" he would shout gleefully as he set off across the ice, to try again at locating the remains of some long-lost expedition from the United States or Denmark.

My parents were eager seekers of remains, and spent inordinate amounts of time listening to the oral histories of Eskimos, hoping for clues to where white men had traveled in past centuries, and where they might have died. My fondest memories are of the excitement and pleasure my parents evinced when they came upon the clothes, the spoons and knives, the lengths of copper wire that the dead had left behind. They were as much children as I then, poking about among the half-gnawed femurs, the metal buttons, the untouched tins of chocolate that had lain so long exposed to the cruel elements of the Frozen North!

Much of the year there is no dawn. I rise in the dark and light the oil lamp, lengthen and trim its wick, and eat sparingly of the dried fish, or the dried blubber, or the dried seal meat that is my ration. Most days I don't feed the dogs. My dog herd has grown, because I have more heart than my poor father ever had, and I find it so difficult to kill the puppies when they're born. Also, I'm not the man my father was: I'm frightened of them. He used to creep so boldly among them as they lay half-buried in the snow, never touching them until he reached the new-whelped bitch, and then he'd pick up the puppies one by one and look at them. The biggest he gave back to her, but the smaller, and the runts, he carried in the shelter of his bearskin parka back to the igloo, where he broke their useless necks with the flick of a gloved finger. Then what feasts we had!

I don't feed the dogs; they forage for themselves, hunting the foxes and seals, the ravens that live on the ice in the darkness;

and there are those among them that have taken over my father's role as the cullers of the litters.

After I break my own fast, I dress warmly, pulling on my leggings and my parka, my fur mukluks and my triple-layer mittens, putting my fox fur mask over my head to protect the flesh of my face. I pick up my guns and my knives, my thongs and ropes, the whip I use when the dogs get too close, and my compass, and am ready to set out.

I shout and scream and sometimes fire the gun to clear the dogs away from the igloo's entrance before I go out. It is dark, unless the moon is up or the stars are bright. I check my compass, and head out in the direction that seems best.

How my parents chose where to go, I never learned. They had their instruments and their charts, and I believe their methods were scientifically derived; but I never learned their ways. They never realized, I think, that I would grow up one day. They never thought to teach me the skills an explorer needs. No reading of instruments, no interpreting of data, no understanding of charts. No recording of digits—although I can read them, I cannot tell you what they mean. I know I have two hands, two eyes, two nostrils, two breasts, and one head; I know no more.

I choose my direction by the wind: I put it at my back. I go where the ice is whole and solid, and avoid the creaking, shifting fields of summer ice.

I may follow the dogs, who wake when I step outside the igloo. They snarl and fight among themselves until they sense my purpose, and then they run in a great pack beside me, leaping over each other, each biting at the hind leg of the one in front of him, barking and howling with the joy of living in the North. But on some days their behavior changes: they might sit still and silent, not moving even when I show my readiness; or they might lead the way themselves, the great white bitch whimpering as she sets off at the head of the pack.

I watch them closely. If they head out with purpose, I follow

in their tracks. But if they wait for my decision, I look for
other guides.

Ravens, the great nightmares of the north, may guide me.
In winter they're black against the ice when they walk, strut-
ting and croaking and stealing bits of raw flesh from the dogs,
or from me. But when they lift off into the dark sky, they're
invisible, and I can only follow them by the sounds they
make, the croaks and creaks that might be their wings moving in the icy air, sounding like the timbers of wooden ships
being slowly crushed and splintered in the shifting ice or like
the cracking and snapping of the ice itself as it grows and
breathes with the sea beneath it. Ravens most often travel in
pairs. If a single raven appears and lingers, it is a sign of
death, or loss. Then I stay inside my igloo.

The choice of direction made, I walk. My parents had a
sledge when I was young, and they tied the dogs to it and
made them pull it, bearing me and mounds of food and furs.
They ran beside it, shouting at the dogs, my father whipping
at them, me strapped to a dead seal and listening in comfort
to the dogs whining and panting and fighting as they ran. In
this way we traveled for hours at a time, my parents shouting,
running behind, the ravens soaring without effort overhead,
and the ice snapping and booming under and ahead and
below. It was a world of ice.

I don't have the control over the animals that my parents
had. The dogs multiply in number, they eat each other, they've
eaten the traces that attached them to the old sledge, they
snap at me and snarl when I come too near. I walk, and the
dogs run beside me, whining. Sometimes I come upon the remains of the sledge where I finally left it, long ago, at the
edge of the sea. I am always surprised to see it. Little of it
remains: some iron nails that my father had salvaged from a
whaler abandoned in the ice, a piece of half-chewed wood
here and there, a page from my mother's records that emerges
from the ice undamaged after years of burial. I sit down on a

bit of board, and close my eyes and imagine that once again I'm tiny, wrapped in furs and strapped to a great sledge pulled by dogs, and my mother is running nearby, screaming, and the wind is behind us.

I dare not stay lost in imagination for long, because the dogs are often hungry.

My parents told of endless herds of caribou, streaming for days from north to south and back again, searching for the lichens that grow on solid ground beyond the floes. My parents never saw them; the oceans of caribou were before their time. They saw not much more than I see now: ungulates numbering in the hundreds, streaming endlessly enough, heedless of my guns. I kill the stragglers, the young that come last in the migration, and let the dogs feed without restraint. Then I take the hide to make clothing for myself, and take enough flesh to feast now and to dry a supply for the coming weeks.

Sometimes I find strange monuments from the journeys of the old explorers; they expended more energy than I can imagine just piling up rocks, and they carved things from wood, thinking they would last as monuments to fallen comrades. Instead they were mostly eaten by angry polar bears, or by me, when I was starving.

At any rate, as I never learned to use the compass, I simply say I'm heading north.

No one asks. I speak to no one.

I do not stop all day, a choice I make of my own free will, a concept my father once explained to me. From time to time I nibble at the dried flesh I carry at all times. I keep my eye on the dogs. The sun is hovering just below the horizon much of the year, and I imagine it moving beside me, along the rim of the earth. My father also explained that the earth has no rim, but I find this hard to credit. What's beyond the edge? He explained that there are strange worlds, like Indiana and Ireland; these are beyond my understanding.

Following in my parents' footsteps as I do, I have no permanent home; I am ever on the move, and build a new snow hut every night. With the knife I removed from my father's dead body, I cut blocks from the snow—blocks as big as I can make them, for the bigger they are, the fewer I need. I drag them one by one to the location of the igloo—always in the thickest part of the ice, or on nearby land, if there is any. I stack them one on top of another, in the traditional shape of an igloo, and make a short tunnel to keep the wind out. When it's finished I crawl inside, leaving the dogs to circle and mark out their own territories.

I light the oil lamp, and the heat from its flame soon fills the ice house and melts a thin film of water on the inner surfaces of the ice chunks: mingling with the moisture of my breath it fills the little shelter with humidity, dripping from the ceiling onto the blankets and onto my face and hair. The moisture makes it easier to breathe again. My chapped and frostbitten nose then bleeds freely, and my lips burn.

Long ago, when I traveled with my mother and father, they built the igloo for the night and then spread upon the floor a large bag made of skins. After eating, they would crawl into it, heaping more furs on top of themselves, and I too would crawl in, snuggling myself down into the bag beside them. The warmth we shared! The heat from their two large bodies was more than sufficient for warming my own little body; their shifting and groaning in the night was my lullaby.

I eat whatever food I have, puppy or seal or caribou flesh, and then I crawl alone into my fur bag and curl around myself, often regretting the lost warmth of my parents. When the oil lamp is extinguished, the moisture in the shelter instantly freezes; I sleep encased in a film of ice, and the ceiling is sealed with ice against the wind. I am often cold, but I have learned to sleep that way.

No human being could survive a night without shelter, but the dogs curl around themselves, fighting for the deepest softest snow, and let the blowing drifts cover them until they lie in little igloos of their own.

I wake in the darkness and listen. The wind screams outside, ice crystals pelt the rounded roof of the igloo like the droppings of the great flocks of migrating snow geese that pass by during certain seasons, dogs whimper in their sleep.

I lie still. I fall asleep again. I wake, and the wind still blows. It is, I judge, ninety miles per; I have no anemometer, but I remember my father announcing the measurement of wind velocity aloud; and when he said, "Ninety miles per! We'll lie abed, my sweet!" and laughed his great laugh and crawled back into the bag beside my mother, the wind sounded the way it sounds now.

I lie abed until it slows, or stops. When finally it's quiet, I have no idea how much time has passed. My father's watch stopped within days after his death, and I never rewound it. Now I sometimes wish I could look at digits on my wrist the way my father did, for he seemed to find great comfort in it. But I gave the watch to a band of traveling natives, who gave me something in return that I've lost.

My parents died of starvation. It was a long winter, and few animals came. We ate the dogs, one by one; first the young ones, then the old ones; then every few days my parents killed one of the good, strong ones. In the end the few remaining dogs cowered and ran when he emerged from the igloo, and would not come close enough for him to chain at night. Still they could not stay away; they were servile beasts. They slunk back in the dark, sniffing around the igloo hoping for discarded remnants of their brothers' and sisters' bodies; they were weak, and found it easier to scavenge than to kill fresh meat. Game was scarce for them, too; they would have eaten us, and tried often enough, but we were faster and smarter. My mother told me this. "We're smarter than the dogs," she said once when I ran to her in fear, a dog having attacked, or snarled, or stared at me. And the proof of our superiority was that we ate them, not they us.

The day came when we could not leave our igloo. We lay weak in the darkness, for we had long ago drunk the oil from our lamp. Our bodies grew colder and colder, and we slipped in and out of consciousness. My mother said some last words, but I couldn't understand them, she mumbled so. She moved restlessly, her muscles jerking in spasm, her cheeks sunken and her bald head moving back and forth ceaselessly on the pillow made of a half-chewed piece of wood, perhaps a bit of spar from an old abandoned whaler. I lay beside her, so that she was between me and my father; and when at last my mother stopped moving altogether, I raised my head to look upon her face one last time and found it awful and fleshless. I looked beyond her to my father, and saw at once that he, too, had ceased to breathe, and lay now with his open mouth a great dark toothless cavern, his sightless eyes filmed over, a glaze of ice covering his beard.

They who had given me life, and had spared me time and again when their own stomachs were shriveled and empty, who had gazed upon my rounded childish limbs with forbearance— now, in death, they made no protest as I took from them what I needed to survive. I never loved them more than when I carved the most nutritious portions, tough and nearly indigestible as they were, from their still-warm flesh and swallowed them, hardly chewing in my haste and hunger. And even as they stiffened beside me, I felt my blood begin to flow, my heart to beat with more vigor, and my will to live strengthen, bringing me, at last, to my feet again.

They were young when they died, perhaps younger than I am now; I have no idea. I have nothing: no calendar, no wristwatch, most of the year no sun, and certainly no society. I know nothing that can be of any interest or any use.

I left their remains in that igloo, taking with me my father's knife, my mother's pencil, the oil lamp, what animal skins remained ungnawed. I pondered long my mother's notebooks, my parents' instruments of measurement and exploration; I took what I could carry, knowing that those things had often been coveted by the bands of natives we sometimes met in our travels. I knew they would be useful to me. And in some way I must have hoped that an understanding of them would come with my maturity, for, though my parents had never intimated as much, I knew instinctively that I would someday be an adult, as they had been. I had no idea what this would mean; and in fact it has meant little, except that I grow tired earlier in a walk, but am stronger than I was. This is a paradox of which I have no understanding.

After my parents died I traveled for a long time, followed by skulking dogs who only after some weeks began to come closer, and run beside me, still looking at me with hungry white eyes, but rarely daring to attack. Perhaps that is what assured me I was approaching maturity; they had often attacked my younger, smaller self, and to this day I bear the scars of their teeth.

I walked and walked, exploring alone, and after some months I came again to the place where I had left my dead parents. The northern summer had come and the igloo had melted, and the bodies of my parents were exposed, decayed, torn, and scattered to the winds and elements, having served as meals for whatever creatures had passed by. I often found bits of them—a fingertip, a nose—and of their strange belongings here and there among the boulders, at the edge of a great river, in the nest of a raven. Even now, from time to time, I find remnants of my parents frozen in ice floes, clearly visible beneath my feet, out of reach until the ice melts, if that time ever comes.

My parents were explorers, but to my knowledge they discovered nothing. They recorded every degree of temperature and of latitude or longitude, every angle of the sun and every change in the direction of the wind; but as far as I know they gave none of this to anyone: no government agency, no anthropologist, no historian of northern exploration, no trader, no library. They recorded it all and lost it in the permafrost. I have seen Arctic foxes carrying my mother's notebooks from place to place, trotting across the niveous landscape, the pages flapping with every step.

I am the child of explorers. My parents were limited in their understanding of the world, and I myself am limited in my understanding of my parents' ways. Since my poor parents died, victims at last of decades of exposure to this land, I have gone on alone. I chart nothing; I leave no record of my unceasing travels.

I long for very little. I have forgotten the languages the natives speak, and when I meet them now—if I cannot avoid their traveling groups—I am wary, and I only take, having nothing left to give in return. My long unused facial muscles lie rigid under my tattered skin; my nearly toothless gums give my thick and heavy tongue no encouragement if it moves in an effort to speak. I have no news; I seek no information. I nod, I accept whatever food they offer—seal, dog, or dark, streaked meats that they don't name—and I go on my way, the dogs whining and slinking behind, covering my traces with their own.

Missionaries

◆

EVERYONE'S astonished that Jenny can still compete when she comes back from her mission.

"Holy cow!" Coach says at the end of her floorwork.

"For Christ's sake, she was in *California*," I say to Wayne. "She can probably surf, too."

"Oh, come on, Willa," Wayne says, watching Coach hug Jenny. "You're just jealous."

"I'm not jealous," I say, but I am, a little. Not just because Jenny's so good at gymnastics, but because she's tan, and she has terrific teeth, and she went on a mission. I don't have any religion. And I have these ugly little square gray teeth that are ready to crumble when I hit twenty-five. It happened to my mom, and it happened to my sister, Elaine. Their teeth started to crumble when they were eating their birthday cakes.

"Okay, Willa," Coach yells. "Let's see your balance beam."

I drop my jacket and go for it.

I'm only marginal on the U team. I'm good at beam, and at uneven bars, but anything else, I'm no great shakes. But I work at it, hard, and Coach thinks I'm honest, so I stay in. I don't win any meets for us, but I don't drag down the scores, either.

Wayne's the one who puts me through my paces. He was an athlete until a car whacked into him out on Route 89 one fall night, when he was jogging. He was wearing glow strips all over his shoes, and he was facing traffic, but this car smashed into him all the same. When Wayne could talk again he said the car aimed right at him. Wayne has to have a reason for the accident, and the best one he could come up with was that somebody was jealous of his success.

So he sits there in his wheelchair and yells at me, and I breathe right, and concentrate, and do what he says. In a way, I do this for him.

"Willa!" Wayne yells. "Use those arms; don't just let them hang!" It's all he can do, yell, his arms hanging there useless.

I had never *heard* of missions when Jenny said she was going on one. She explained it to me, but I still can't picture it.

"How on earth can you convince people about God?" I said.

"You'd be surprised how eager some of them are to hear it," she said. Then she shrugged. "I can't really explain how it works. You feel the spirit, and it enters you, and you help them to feel it too."

"It sounds like sex," I said, trying to make a joke of it.

"Well, it *is*," she said, making her eyes completely round. "It's the same sort of thing, the same joy and sharing you experience in sex. It flows through you and into your heart. You can't even begin to imagine it, Willa, until you've felt it."

It gave me the creeps, to see how eager she looked. I trusted her information on sex just about as much as her information on religion, so I wished her luck in California and went to the library.

I couldn't help thinking about it, though. When Wayne and I have sex, I'm the one who has to be on top, and put him in the right position, and do all the moves, so I have to stay limber—so he can please me, he says.

"I feel the spirit," I say to Wayne that night. "I can help you to feel it too."

"You don't really understand a thing about religion, do you," he says, looking at me.

"No," I say.

"At least it's a feminine sport," my sister says. Elaine spends a lot of time, a *lot* of time, gluing fake nails onto her real ones, and having her bikini line waxed. She's not brainless—she's a tax attorney—but her spare time goes into grooming.

Coach thinks she's spectacular. "Holy shit," I heard him say the first time she dropped by practice. "God's gift to coaches."

Elaine's had her little gray teeth capped, and she has white-blond hair that she got from her father, who isn't my father, and she can actually walk in three-inch heels without looking like her ankles will break.

"So you're Coach," she says, and she gives him a quick up-and-down, looking right at his ring.

He gives her pure down, right into her cleavage. Coach isn't bad himself. No belly, no hips, plenty of hair.

So Coach and Elaine are going out together. "If you tell *anyone*," Elaine says, "*anyone*, Willa, he'll lose his job. I mean *anyone*."

"Even Wayne?" I say, just to say it.

"My God, Willa," Elaine says. She stares at me and shakes her head. "Leave Wayne out of this, will you?"

What Elaine does is her business, and what I do is mine.

"So Willa," Jenny says, "are you and Wayne getting married?" She says it casually in the locker room while we're getting dressed.

I shrug. "We haven't really talked about it," I say, though that's not strictly true. "Why?"

"Oh, I don't know." She's very interested in her shoelaces. "You just seem so devoted to him."

"You make me sound like a golden retriever," I say.

She doesn't laugh, though; she blushes. "I didn't mean that," she says. "It's just, oh, since I've been back, I see things differently." She looks right at me then, buttoning her shirt. "There's so much *out* there."

She's a lot like Elaine—she's blond, she's perfectly groomed, even her sweat is attractive. But Jenny's pure.

"Did you like California?" I say.

She frowns a little, thinking. "I can't decide," she says. "I was so homesick. And it's so different." She shakes her head, and reaches up to start brushing her hair. "No, not really. It's beautiful, but I wouldn't want to live there."

"Why not?" I say. "It's supposed to be paradise, isn't it?"

"It's supposed to be," Jenny says, "but it's so full of temptation." She laughs. "I don't mean to sound like fire and brimstone," she says, "but it's hard to tell where you are out there. You can't tell what's good and what's bad."

I picture California, the sun always out, oranges growing on trees, everybody blond. "Maybe it's better," I say. "Maybe if you don't tell people about evil they won't think of it themselves."

"No," Jenny says. "That much I know. You have to warn them, or they're goners."

"What's that in your middle?" Wayne says, peering at me. "Flab?"

"Where?" I stand up and look at myself in the mirror. "There's no flab there."

He's grinning. "Had you worried, didn't I?" he says. "Can't hide anything from me."

He's always a little mean when he gets back from therapy.

"Walker Petty is such a *loser*," Wayne says. Walker is Wayne's physical therapist. He takes Wayne into the pool, works his legs, lugs him out and drapes him over a big barrel, and rolls him around the floor. It's supposed to keep Wayne's muscles from atrophying, but they've atrophied anyway.

"You mad at him or something?" I say, because he does sound mad.

"Shit," Wayne says. "He's wasted his life."

"He coulda been a contender," I say.

"Shut up, Willa," Wayne says.

Walker and Wayne played basketball together in college. Walker got an offer from the Celtics, but he didn't go. He went to school in PT, and now he works down at the Rehab Institute.

"He should have gone to medical school," Wayne says. "He should have done something with his life."

"What's wrong with PT?" I say.

"Anybody who spends his life around gimps is a loser," Wayne says.

I'm not sure it's good to know what your coach does in his spare time.

"Okay, Willa, let's see what you can do," Coach says, his eyes narrowed as if he suspects me of something. But I can't remember how he used to look at me.

I spring out to the bars. The rest of the team claps—it's Coach's rule, that we cheer each other on. He doesn't want us competing against each other. He wants us to think we're in this together.

I turn back toward them and smile hugely with my little gray teeth, sticking my arms up in a V. Coach is watching me, standing with his hands on his hips and no expression on his face.

I hate knowing what's on his mind.

It's not that I see a lot of Elaine. We have holiday dinners at my mom's house, sometimes we go to the same party or run into each other at a movie. Usually Wayne's with me, so we just say hi.

But with this Coach thing, she comes to home meets. She sits near the top of the bleachers, always in nylons, showing off a lot of thigh. When I'm out on the floor it's as if there's a spotlight on her white-blond hair, and whenever I face the audience it's Elaine that I see; not Coach, who has to stay down on the bench; not Wayne, who's parked in his chair over at the end of the bleachers.

I know it's the same for them. Coach's back is all prickles, knowing she's up there behind him, and his breath comes shorter.

Wayne's eyes are on me, but by the end of the evening his whole helpless body, strapped into his chair, has shifted, ever so slightly. He yells for me, but from the corner of his eye he watches the glow of my sister's hair.

Elaine sits up there and never takes her eyes off me. She sees every move I make, sees every mistake, knows all there is to know about my body. Her eyes bore right into me.

I think to myself, right as I start my routine, This is for you, Wayne.

Jenny and I have started running together. "The one thing I could do," she says between breaths, "in California, is run."

"You seem devoted to gymnastics," I say. People are sitting half nude all over campus, studying and chewing gum in the sun. I know what's really on their minds: sex, sex, sex.

"I am," she says.

She never hears anything that isn't smack on the surface of what I say. I think she's stupid, but I admire her. No hidden meanings, no secrets, no insinuations. Her life seems so straightforward. She needs no answers, because she's not worried about the questions.

"What motivates you?" I say.

"Love, I think," she says. "I want to do good."

"Do well," I can't help saying.

She laughs. "No, I mean, do good in the *world*," she says.

We slow down and then stop, panting, wiping the sweat off our faces. Her skin is as uncomplicated as her soul. We sit down under a honey locust tree. I blow my nose, but Jenny doesn't need to blow hers. I can see her future: she will not get flabby or wrinkled; she will just become a little blurred.

"Willa," she says, "what are you going to do after graduation?" I'm graduating, but because she went on a mission for two years, Jenny has another year to go.

"Oh, I'll still be in town," I say. "I'll come and cheer at every meet."

Coach calls me in. "What are your plans, Willa?" Coach says.

"Are you calling all of us in, or what?" I say. "Is this part of your job?"

"I'm sending my girls, my athletes, out into the world," Coach says. "I want to know what they think I've prepared them for."

"What motivates you, Coach?" I say.

He looks thoughtful. He's not a stupid man; rumor has it he's one of the heavy Mensas, maybe 170. "Motivation is a complex issue," Coach says.

"Well, for me, it's love," I say.

Coach blinks at me. "When do you start?" he says.

When Wayne got smashed by the car on Route 89 he had an out-of-body experience. As in all verified OOBEs, he floated above himself, looking down at the accident scene, and then a long shaft of white light hit him, and he started rising toward its source. His dead eighth-grade wrestling coach met him at the top of the light shaft.

"Go back," he said to Wayne. "It's not your time."

So Wayne had to float back down again and hunt up his

body, which by this time had been transferred over to the surgical suite at Community Hospital. He slipped back into it in the middle of an operation to reconnect one of his feet at the ankle.

He opened his eyes just to make sure he was in the right place.

"Jesus Christ," the anesthetist said, and for a minute Wayne thought something had gone wrong.

Wayne and Elaine were in college, but I was in eighth grade at the time, and after I heard about Wayne's OOB experience I started going to the wrestling meets. Instead of watching the boys struggle with each other on the floor, I watched Mr. Hessler, the coach who had replaced Wayne's dead one.

Mr. Hessler sweated and swore and breathed heavily, and shouted at the boys on his team. He leaned forward all the time. I thought that if anyone could draw me out of my body, it would be Mr. Hessler.

Once during the school day I walked through the double doors of the room where Mr. Hessler taught Shop. It smelled of raw wood.

"Yeah?" Mr. Hessler said when he saw me.

"I just wanted you to know I'm a big fan," I said.

"Yeah?" he said, leaning forward. "Biggie wow."

Jenny's the star of the team. Watching her is a delight to the eye and to the senses: she even smells good as she runs past out onto the floor. Some performers—like me—you watch sideways with your lids half lowered, ready to close if she starts to slip or you see that her timing's off and she's about to hit the floor shoulder first, breaking her neck, paralyzing herself. Not Jenny. You have no fears with Jenny.

We get big audiences these days. Last year we got our relatives, our roommates, and the losers who have nothing better to do on Tuesday nights than watch girls in tights. Now that Jenny's back, though, we're an attraction. We get strangers, non-university people, and members of Jenny's church, which means the stands are full. We have policemen directing traffic before and after the meets.

"They worship you," I say in the locker room, after Jenny's racked up a 10-9-9 score.

"Oh, not *me*," she says. She pretends it's the team, or the sport, or the school that they worship.

I think she knows the truth. Is she lying? Is that a sin? I look closely at her backside as she heads for the shower. She's pink and undimpled.

"Jenny?" I say.

She turns around, clutching her towel in front of her. "You were terrific out there," I say. "You know it."

"It was a good night," she says. "Hard work pays off."

I can't let it go. "You really had spirit," I say.

She nods. "That too," she says.

Sometimes I drive past Elaine's apartment. Sometimes I park on the street and sit in the car, looking up at her windows. She's fastidious about closing the curtains, but I know when she's not alone. I can see Elaine and Coach together, Coach taking off his striped shirt, unfastening his black leather belt, letting his pants drop to the floor. Elaine letting her bathrobe fall beside them.

Coach was an athlete. He's still a vigorous man. I can see him picking her up off the floor, lifting her in his arms, arranging her the way he wants her. He has thick, muscular legs, and sometimes he stands over her, lifting weights, jumping up and grabbing onto the light fixture, chinning himself as she watches from below. He drops to the floor and does a dozen pushups, then rolls into a headstand. Elaine can't move. Coach raises himself onto his hands and walks on them over to the bed.

I know when Coach is there, because he parks his car in the street. I park behind it. Elaine is something like a slug,

I think; a large pink slug that lies inert, waiting to have something done to it.

I do things to his car. I try to let the air out of his tires, but when I get the little cap off, nothing happens. I scoop up a lot of rotting leaves from the gutter and paste them on his windshield. The next time, I bring a bar of Dial that I took from Jenny's locker when she was in the shower and write COACH on the windshield. GOD WAS HERE I write backwards, on the back window, so he can read it in his rearview window as he drives away.

"What's gotten into you?" Wayne says. We're at the Village Inn, late at night, eating banana cream pie. With an early forkful I got some whipped cream on his nose, and I've left it there. I hate myself for the pleasure I get looking at it.

"Pie," I say.

"Something's going on with you, Willa," Wayne says. "I want to know what it is."

I have powers that Wayne doesn't begin to suspect. In addition to tonight's whipped cream, I've used gravy, poppyseeds, egg yolk, and thin pieces of spinach that wrap themselves around one of his teeth, making him look like a goon when he smiles. There are other things: boogers, unzipped flies, even the part in his hair.

I never used to be this way.

"Honey," I say, holding out the last bit of pie, "what are you talking about?"

"You eat it," he says. "I don't think you love me any more."

It occurs to me I might tell him about Elaine and Coach. What would he do if he knew? Nothing! There's nothing he could do.

"You're the one," I say, "who doesn't want to get married."

"Yet," he says. "Not yet." He looks hard at me, narrowing his eyes. His facial muscles, his eyelids, his nostrils are very mobile, very expressive. It's the only way he can reach out and grab me. "I don't trust you enough."

"What do you want me to do?" I say. Seven years I've been with him, ever since he was at the Rehab Institute and Elaine dumped him.

"It's not what you *do*," he says. "It's what you fucking *are*."

"I don't think we should see each other for a while," I say, looking into the mirror. "Maybe we should see other people."

I look back at myself. "Sure," I say. "Easy for you to say."

The thing is, who would want to see Wayne? Who wants to take on the job of feeding him, washing him, lugging him in and out of cars and wheelchairs and beds? Who wants to do gymnastics just to get a little sex?

"I want to see other people," I say. But that's not true either.

"Anybody who spends their life around gimps is a loser," I say. I have to smile at that.

Jenny started out premed, but when she got back from her mission she switched to business. "I think it's the way to do large-scale good in the world," she says. "A doctor can save a life, or let someone die peacefully. But it's the large corporations that have the most lasting effects."

She means this in a pure and righteous way.

"Some people would say the corporation is corrupt by definition," I say.

"That's not what I believe," she says. There's a little frown in her forehead. "With enough of the right thinking, and with good organization, a corporation can save the world. If I didn't believe that, Willa, I might just give up."

I wonder what would make Jenny give up. Would she even recognize corruption?

"Some people might say," Jenny says, "that the church I belong to is itself a large corporation."

"In the business of saving souls," I say.

She nods eagerly. "You see? That's language they can *understand*. And in their terms, it's exactly right! Putting salvation into the corporate mentality. *That's* the work I want to do."

"What is the nature of evil?" I say to Jenny. "What is a sin?"

"Pretty heavy questions, Willa," she says, and she keeps running.

Coach calls me in. "Wipe that look off your face," he says. "Stop trying to be a fucking saint."

"Why don't you grow up?" Elaine says. "You could be so pretty if you'd try."

I don't call Wayne, and he doesn't call me. For all I know, he's left his body for good. I don't worry about him. He's got home nursing care eight hours a day.

"I wasn't kidding," I say to Jenny. "I want to understand the nature of sin."

"I'm not the one to talk to," she says, though I disagree. She's almost glowing, sitting there in her carrel in the business library. If I were the CEO of an international corporation, and Jenny ran in to tell me how to make money for the greater glory of God, I would fall to my knees before her. I would hand her the keys to my kingdom.

"What was it like, being on a mission?" I say. "Did you feel powerful? Were you scared?"

Jenny taps her pen against her teeth. "I was so scared," she says. "I was afraid no one would believe me. I was afraid I wouldn't know what to say when people opened the door. But every time, when the door would open, I could feel the spirit enter me. I didn't have to worry, I didn't even have to think. Someone else was speaking through me."

I'm getting desperate. Everywhere I look people's bodies are like swinging doors, spirits going in and out, people exiting and getting entered right and left.

Can I tell her about Elaine and Coach? Would she hear me? I close my eyes for a minute, and then I open them. "I've been thinking of getting married," I say, and watch her.

She looks up at me, her little teeth gleaming between her parted lips. She's short of breath. "It bears thinking about," she says. "But I'm not the one to ask."

"I might go to business school," I tell Coach.

"That's terrific, Willa," he says. He stares up at me, his sweaty face nearly as immobile as Wayne's lower body.

"Or I might not," I say. "It's a decision I haven't made."

"You want some advice?" Coach says.

"Not really," I say, although I've begun to suspect I'm looking for answers.

"Come on," he says, "it's free." He lets down the barbell he's been holding over his chest and gets up from the bench. He comes around to the front of his desk and sits on the edge of it, crossing his legs at the ankle, folding his arms, and leans forward at me.

I pull my hands out from where I've been pressing them between my knees, and I fold my arms and push back in my chair. "Price is right," I say.

"You're not doing yourself any favors by your attitude," he says.

I wait, but he's stopped. "Is that it?" I say.

"Willa, I'm trying to be your friend," he says. He slips off the desk and onto his knees at my feet. He puts his hands on either arm of the chair as if he's trapped me. "I want to help you, Willa," he whispers.

"I'm waiting," I say. His breath is sweet, like grape juice.

"You can do better than Wayne," Coach says. He closes his eyes and shakes his head. "Get out. See the world. There's more to life than"—his eyes pop open, and he swings one arm out to his side—"this!"

"Coach," I say, and I lean forward, "you have helped me more than you know."

He puts his hand on my thigh. "Willa," he says, "you are a very lucky woman."

I'm not God's gift to the gymnastics team, but I pull my own weight. I win my share of competitions, I have terrific muscle tone, and I'm a good loser, too.

"Elaine," I say as she's giving me a lift home from our mom's house, "I think I'm falling in love."

"Nonsense," she says, and she tosses her cigarette out the car window. "You've got a future."

"Don't you want to know who the guy is?" I say.

"It doesn't matter to me, sweetie," she says.

I call Wayne.

"What do you want?" he says.

"Advice," I say.

"Do it," he says. "It's so important to you, do it, for God's sake."

"When can I see you?" I say.

He doesn't answer for a long time. Then he says, "You're so fucking happy."

"It's my nature, Wayne," I say. "Coach can't stand it either."

"That slob," he says.

"Tonight's the last meet of the season," I say, putting my lips very close to the receiver.

"God," Wayne says in a husky voice. "I'm coming."

It's the last meet of the season, and I'm sitting right behind Coach, looking at the place on the top of his head where his hair is beginning to thin out. I know Elaine is staring down at me from the top row of the stand. Wayne is in his usual place, his body twisted toward the floor.

Jenny's up on the beam. We clapped as she ran out, and she sprang up as if she weighs nothing—as if she could be whipped away in a gust of wind. She rolls the length of the beam, then twists, stands up, cartwheels back across it. She stands and faces us, and her face is radiant, suffused with some heavenly light. She holds her arms out wide. She lowers

herself to the beam until she is stretched out full length, looking straight up. Slowly her feet rise toward the ceiling, then
lower toward her head; her hips lift up, and her legs stretch
back over her body, till her toes are on the beam. I can see
the muscles in her calves, long and unmoving as she holds
her position.

Then, fast and smooth, she swings her legs back over her
body and down on either side of the beam, sitting up, rocking
forward, her arms straight out at her sides and her face ecstatic.
Without moving her arms she swings her legs up and makes
her body a V, and then she leaps off and is done. We applaud
like crazy.

"Willa!" Coach shouts. "Move!"

The body is God's temple. I run out to the beam, light as a
feather, and leapfrog up. I roll, and balance, and turn in
midair, and everything is perfect. I am in perfect condition. I
have wonderful muscle tone.

It is my best performance ever.

"Good God," Coach says as I spring back to the mat.

I can feel my eyes shining and the blood flowing freely
through every part of my body.

"Nice," Elaine calls, and she slides her eyes over me.

"Oh, Willa!" Jenny says. She is clinging to Coach.

"Fucking A!" Wayne shouts, and as I watch, the little
finger on his left hand moves.

I run across the floor toward him, but Jenny is there before
me. "Oh, Wayne!" she says, and she sinks down in front of
him and grabs the moving finger. "Oh, I've prayed for this!"
She buries her face in his lap, but he doesn't respond.

How can he? He feels nothing down there. He just looks
up at me, smiling. "Great routine, Willa," he says.

Jenny looks up at me too, and her cheeks are shiny and
wet. She whispers, "I'm so happy for you."

I put my hand on her head, and then let my fingers drift
through her soft blond hair. "Thank you," I say, and then I

turn away, back toward the floor, where the next performer is approaching the beam.

"Let's go!" I shout, raising my arms in benediction. "Let's see another miracle!" I feel the blood flowing through my arms, heating up, racing faster and faster in its endless, inescapable track. I think I've got the spirit, and it feels like love.

Love in the Winter

◆

"**I** AM a turkey," Vishnu says happily.

Dolly looks across the table at him. If anything, he's a grackle, she thinks; he's sleek, his glossy hair so dark it has purple highlights, his eyes bright above his beaky nose.

"Stuffed?" Jimmy says.

"Ah! You have gotten it!" Vishnu beams at Jimmy, and moves around the table, pouring more wine.

It is the first turkey Dolly has ever cooked, and her first Thanksgiving in the city, away from home. She likes Thanksgiving, and she likes having her friends together—her new roommate, Belle, and her co-worker Jimmy, and Vishnu, who has taken to American holidays and to the role of host as if they were made for him.

She wonders what she would look like with a red dot in the middle of her forehead.

"It is a mirror-image holiday," Vishnu says. "I am the father, and Jimmy is the mom."

They all look out the dining room window, which looks into the dining room of an apartment in the next building. Dolly and Belle have watched the people who live there eat meals, walk through the room naked, and threaten each other with knives; but not once have the neighbors looked back at them.

Today the neighbors are sitting at Thanksgiving dinner, their dining room an exact replica of Dolly's. They could almost be a mirror image; only the faces are different.

"Dolly is that old fat uncle," Jimmy says. "Belle's the tot."

"Perhaps this is a mirror which reveals our true images," Vishnu says. "Once a year, on the national day of thanking, we see ourselves clearly."

"A toast!" Dolly says. "To ourselves, as others see us!"

They raise their glasses toward the window. They drink, and the mirror-image family continues to shovel forkloads of turkey and potatoes into their mouths. The mother spoons something mashed into the mouth of the infant.

"This is not good," Vishnu says. He is still looking out the window.

"It's my mom's recipe," Belle says.

"No, no, the pumpkin pie is very tasty," he says. "No, it is the uncle who is not doing well."

They turn to look through the window as the uncle stands up, coughing, covering his mouth with his napkin. He waves wildly at his throat.

"He's choking!" Jimmy says.

Vishnu jumps from his chair and runs to the window. "Heimlich!" he shouts, beating on the glass. "Do the Heimlich!"

The father has dropped his fork and is pounding on the uncle's back.

"No!" Vishnu shouts.

The father throws his arms around the uncle's big stomach and squeezes hard, again and again. The uncle's face has turned red and is growing darker. He is gagging, a stream of saliva pouring from his mouth. He sags against the table, then falls to the floor, his hand catching a plate and bringing its load of potatoes and gravy over on top of him. His face is now purple. The father and mother yank on his feet, turn him over, and push on his back. The uncle's body shudders, convulsing. The mother runs from the room. The father continues to beat on the uncle's back, tears running down his face.

"My god," Belle whispers.

The baby laughs and throws a handful of peas on the floor.

"I should have saved him," Vishnu says.

The paramedics have come, and they have gone, taking the uncle's body with them. A couple of policemen appeared, took notes, patted the mirror-image mother's shoulder, and went away.

"What could you do?" Dolly says. "We don't even know them. You couldn't have reached them in time."

"I have failed," he says, plucking at the arm of the overstuffed chair.

"Vishnu, you can't save the world," Belle says. "They wouldn't even look at us."

Jimmy sits down and puts his arm around Vishnu.

I should have done that, Dolly thinks.

"You must have seen many people die," Jimmy says. "It doesn't get easier, does it?"

Vishnu shakes his head. "Every time, I take the entire responsibility. I have the skill to save lives, and yet I fail to do it. God will punish me."

"Poohpah," Belle says. "It's sad and all, but everybody has to go sometime. What's better than kicking off in the middle of Thanksgiving dinner?"

"I'd wait till after the pumpkin pie," Jimmy says.

"We cannot choose," Vishnu says.

"You are so beautiful and fair," Vishnu sometimes whispers to Dolly. "You make me hot."

He is tall for an Indian, and heading for plumpness. They have nothing in common, and he has been betrothed for a long time to a beautiful Indian woman who is in medical school in England. Someday she will come here and marry him. He never speaks of her.

As she kisses Vishnu, Dolly thinks, Am I in love?

"It's such a waste of time," she says. "What do I want out of it?" Dolly and Jimmy are sitting in their office on the twenty-third floor and staring out at the lake.

Jimmy pops the end of his Twinkie into his mouth. Then he leers, as best he can with a mouthful of white cream. But before he can speak, the phone rings, and he reaches for it. "Fly By Night Office Supply," he says, and she gasps before she sees he has his hand on the button. The phone rings again, and he releases it. "Office Automation Projects," he says, and she sighs with relief.

They plunge right into Christmas. "I love the United States," Vishnu says as they watch Santa roll down State Street. "We go from one holiday to the next!" He waves vigorously at Santa, who tosses a handful of peppermints at him.

"Don't eat that," a woman says, slapping a candy cane out of a small boy's hand. "You don't know what it's laced with."

"Look," Dolly says. "Santa is black."

"This is a great country!" Vishnu says. He seizes her and gives her a kiss.

They move with the rest of the city's population down the street to Marshall Field's windows. "These little villages," Vishnu says. "I am gazing at them for hours." He stands with his face nearly flat against the glass, watching tiny skaters gliding across a mirror. Cunning wee houses and flocked mini-trees surround the looking-glass lake, and from the speakers above the window a tinny "Little Town of Bethlehem" competes with the "Silent Night" a Salvation Army band plays in the street.

"I am loving these angels," Vishnu says. He kisses the plate-glass window and sighs. A nearby mother pulls her

child on to the next window. "I am on call now," Vishnu says
to the window. "Good-bye, precious skaters!"

They make their way slowly down under the street, and at a
turnstile Vishnu kisses Dolly good-bye, and she watches him
move with a crowd toward the southbound train that will take
him to the Emergency Room at St. J's. She pushes through
the doors of the next northbound train along with a thousand
other people. The door slides shut, and she is carried home.

Belle works for the state, and along with three thousand
other state employees she has gotten an invitation to the governor's third inaugural ball in January.

"Dolly," Belle says, "do you think Vishnu would go to the
Governor's Ball with me?"

Dolly hasn't really known Belle very long, and she doesn't
like her mouth, which she thinks is too big. Also, she has bad
posture.

"Belle," she says, "Vishnu and I are going out together."

"But you're not serious about him," Belle says. "It's not
like you're planning to get married or anything."

Dolly tries to think of a reason why Belle should not invite
Vishnu to go to a party two hundred miles away, where they
will have to stay overnight in a motel, but she can't. Belle's
right; Dolly's not serious about Vishnu.

"It would make me uncomfortable," she says.

"But it's not like it would *mean* anything," Belle says, looking at her with her big lips pursed, as if Dolly is being unreasonable.

"Why don't you take me?" Dolly says.

Belle laughs as if she's said another crazy thing.

The Governor's Ball! Dolly sees herself in a long, flowing
gown, being swept across the crowded dance floor by the governor himself—who, even though he's a Republican, is not
unattractive. He's wearing a tuxedo. Her gown is . . . red. She
doesn't trip on it, though it's floor-length; in the governor's

arms, she is a superb dancer, waltzing, fox-trotting, even— the crowd stands back and applauds—tangoing.

"My friend Carlos and I have an open relationship," Jimmy says. "We know we can't satisfy all of each other's needs." He breathes on the glass, but it's double-paned, and it doesn't steam up.

"Is there something wrong with me?" Dolly says. "Why does it make me feel so bad?"

"You're possessive, that's all," Jimmy says. "Dolly, you don't love him, do you?"

"No," she says, though her heart skips a beat at the word. "But it's the idea of it."

"My advice," Jimmy says, "is, don't make a fuss. Don't get clingy. Anyway, I don't think you have anything to worry about. Belle isn't his type."

But she doesn't feel better. Will she ever get over this possessiveness problem?

Dolly and Belle sit at the back of the bus, watching the city slide by. It snowed a week ago, and what's left is a gray sludge that builds up on the bottoms of cars and then falls off in solid chunks that lie in the street waiting to knock even Buicks out of alignment.

"Have you ever watched him play before?" Belle says. They're on their way to watch Vishnu's underwater hockey team compete in the holiday tournament.

"No," Dolly says.

"This should be fun," Belle says.

"Miss," says a black man across the aisle. "You might want to change seats. We be going by the projects pretty soon."

"Change seats?" Dolly says.

"They see white people, sometimes they shoot," the man says.

"Oh," she says. "Thank you." They move across the aisle.

The bus picks up speed as they pass the vast sad buildings, many of their windows vacant and boarded up. Here and there a bright green or orange or pink shade is drawn down.

"You be okay now," the man says when he gets off. "Next time, take the express."

The wind is pouring out of the west as they walk from the bus stop to the Natatorium. Inside, they stand still, wiping the steam off their glasses. A guard sitting behind a desk watches them.

"Can you tell us where the underwater hockey tournament is?" Belle says.

He points at a stairway. They go up, and through a double door, and are on a balcony, a gallery that runs all around a huge room. They go to the railing and look down at the swimming pool.

It's full of men: Vishnu's team and the opposition. They are moving around on the bottom of the pool in slow motion, their wavery hockey sticks moving slowly in front of them. Now and then one of them pushes off from the bottom and his head pops out of the water. Dolly and Belle can hear him take a giant, gasping breath, and then he goes under again.

They are the only audience. "Is that the puck?" Belle says.

"I think that's Vishnu," Dolly says. "With the yellow trunks." He's the only athletic Indian she knows; in fact he's the only Indian she knows at all.

Someone pops up and sucks air, and goes down again.

"Vishnu must have tremendous lung capacity," Belle says.

Dolly pictures Vishnu's tan and hairless chest, filled with lungs so large that his tiny heart is squashed between them, atrophied, hardly able to beat.

Thousands of people in their winter coats are caroling to the animals at the zoo. They used to go from cage to cage, singing a different song for each species. Now caroling is so popular the singers can only sway and turn in place to face another habitat. Carolers near the sea lions can't get near the big cats; the people surrounding the rain forest sing only to the primates.

Vishnu and Dolly stand next to the polar bear window. The only bear they can see is the one with the skin disease, who has lost all his fur; he swoops down through the water, coming at them head first, then makes a U-turn that exposes his big black testicles, and shoves off from the glass with the smooth black pads of his hind feet.

They sing to him about the Virgin Birth. Dolly thinks, Can he hear us underwater? Are our human voices audible? Maybe he thinks it's a sudden paradise of polar winds, the passing of caribou, the bellows of elephant seals. A perfect, brief gift for a polar bear at Christmas.

Or is she mixing her poles?

"We are all good-natured," Vishnu shouts into her ear during a pause in the singing. "Happy Americans, establishing new rituals."

She tries not to think about the polar bear, whose own ritual never varies. Surface to window, window to surface. Instead she thinks ahead to the cider and doughnuts planned for the lion house at three o'clock. How will they get there through this crowd? How will they all fit in? Will there be any cider left?

Belle is going to her mother's, in Kankakee, for Christmas.

"Have a good time," Dolly says, standing in the hall, watching her lug the suitcase down the stairs to the front door.

Belle looks back up at her, smiling. Her lips are wide, but still her gums show above her large, horsey teeth. "I will," she says.

On Christmas Eve Vishnu spends the night. Dolly has never asked Vishnu what his religion is; she's afraid she'll insult him by saying the wrong thing. Is it the one that worships many-armed ladies in see-through pantaloons? Or does he worship an elephant? She's been to his studio apartment, which is a small room filled by a massive waterbed with a mirrored canopy. She looked around, but there were no shrines, no framed pictures of cows.

Vishnu gives her *The Poetry of Robert Frost*. She gives him a painting she found downtown in a gallery, a scene of State Street in the rain. It is an original, but it was not, of course, expensive.

"Oh, Dolly!" Vishnu says, and he puts his arms around her and squeezes. "If I go into private practice, you will decorate my office!"

Vishnu is on call, of course, and after Christmas breakfast he has to go down to St. J's. He stands combing his hair in front of the mirror, and she sits on the bed to watch him.

Her bedroom window looks across an alley into an upstairs window in the Japanese Christian Church. On Sunday mornings a dozen little Japanese children come to church school in this room, and they are there today, too.

"Look at those children," she says. "They're all so happy."

Vishnu comes over to look. "They are all Down's syndrome children," he says. "Little mongoloids."

She looks closely, and he's right. She's shocked that she hadn't realized it. "Oh, Vishnu," she says, "why is everything so sad?"

"What is sad?" he says. He goes back to the mirror and adjusts his tie. "You are like this orthopod at St. J's. He says, 'Singh, why do you expend your energy on these jungle bunnies?' I tell him, 'They are all children of God.'"

On New Year's Eve it snows, and it keeps snowing for days. The city is paralyzed. The trains don't run, the airport is closed, the highways are clogged with snow. Downtown hotels are full of people who abandoned their cars on Lake Shore Drive and trudged through the blizzard to book a room.

Belle is stuck with her mother in Kankakee, so Dolly has

the apartment to herself. She dances through the rooms singing. She even dances in the dining room; the mirror-image family doesn't look over at her.

She calls Vishnu, who has been trapped at St. J's. "It is a party!" Vishnu says. "All doctors, all nurses and orderlies, even patients—we are celebrating the new year for days!" There is, indeed, raucous laughter in the background, and a snuffly sound, as if Vishnu has put his hand over the mouthpiece. "I must go," he says, suddenly loud in her ear. "I am needed!" There's a phlegmy snort, and Vishnu giggles a high, excited giggle and hangs up.

I shouldn't have called him, Dolly thinks. I should always let him call me. She no longer feels like dancing. *Is* she in love with Vishnu? If only he would call her back and say he wishes she were there.

Her car is buried in snow up to the rearview mirror. All the cars on the street are buried, and there's no sign that snowplows have been by. There would be no place for them to push the snow, anyway; both curbs are solid with snow-covered cars.

Dolly trudges through the snow until she hits a major street that *has* been plowed. She walks in it for a long time, and when she finds herself in front of a theater, she buys a ticket and goes in.

She watches love, murder, intrigue, and sudden death, and although she can't follow the story, she cries for two hours. When she comes out it's after midnight, and there are almost no other people on the streets.

She starts walking north on Halsted Street. There's a great commotion in the next block, and as she gets closer she sees that here there are people, and snowplows, and tow trucks. There are blinding lights aimed at the street, and the whole block is as bright as a movie set.

A police car is cruising up and down, and as it passes her the policeman peers out through the window, his face a white blur. His voice booms out into the night through a loudspeaker.

"PLEASE MOVE YOUR CARS," it echoes. "HALSTED STREET IS BEING PLOWED."

It's true; tow trucks are hauling away the parked cars, and snowplows are scooping huge piles of snow into the backs of pickup trucks, which are driving away with it.

"ALL CARS PARKED ON HALSTED WILL BE TOWED!" the policeman shouts.

Dolly never meant to be walking up Halsted at one in the morning, but she feels safe with the police there. She walks in the street, watching out for large vehicles. The policeman is getting more and more excited, his voice getting higher as he drives back and forth. "PLEASE MOVE YOUR CARS!" he shouts.

As she turns the corner onto Clark, she hears him scream, "ALL CARS PARKED ON HALSTED STREET WILL BE DESTROYED!"

Walking is dangerous; everyone decides that, if the city's not going to plow the streets, *they* won't shovel their sidewalks. People have to climb over mountains of frozen snow, slide down the other side into deeply rutted and ankle-threatening paths, take their bones in their hands when they cross the icy streets.

Mobility is severely limited. Now that they're needed so badly, the trains and the buses break down often, or are delayed by the huge crowds squeezing into and out of them.

Vishnu's been stuck on the south side since New Year's. He says it's all he can do to struggle from his apartment to St. J's and back. "We are in crisis mode!" he says cheerfully. "This snow is making men crazy about their wives!"

"So they come to the hospital?" Dolly says.

"Oh, the many bruises, the broken arms!" Vishnu says, and laughs. "It is a sorry thing, love in the winter."

Dolly listens to the click of the phone as Vishnu hangs up. Sometimes she wonders just what Vishnu means when he speaks of love.

At lunchtime she and Jimmy go up to the post office to pick up their mail. They climb over the grimy mountain of ice, avoiding the frozen puke, to reach the bus. The doors whoosh open, and the driver says, "Come on along with us! Come ride the Happy Bus!"

"Jesus Christ," Dolly mutters.

"We don't mind if we do! We'll come along with you!" Jimmy warbles, and hops up the steps. She climbs up behind him.

"Never mind the snow! Just disregard that woe! Let's sing a happy song, as we drive along!" the bus driver chants; and he starts to sing. "Get your coat, and grab your hat, leave your troubles on the doorstep. Just direct your feet—"

And the whole bus chimes right in, the bundled-up, armpit-smelling, bad-breath crowd, "TO THE SUNNY SIDE OF THE STREET!" They lurch and sing, stop and let in another bewildered newcomer, whip around corners and harmonize as they go. At stoplights they screech to a standstill and the fat driver jumps up to face them, conducting, beaming, his corn-rowed hair glistening with oil. They clap and sing in unison. He slides back into his seat just as the traffic begins to move.

Whenever somebody gets off, the driver says to them, "The Lord has brought you here, safe with all of us; God bless, and come again, to ride the Happy Bus!"

"Phew," Dolly says, as she and Jimmy stumble down the steps and back to the street.

"Here," Jimmy says, handing her the cardboard box he's brought to carry the mail. "Put this on your head."

She does.

He takes her hand and leads her down the street. All she can see is her feet, straight down, inching their way across the ice patches.

"Help this woman," Jimmy is saying. "Please, help her. She has a box on her head."

Belle is hardly ever home. "Busy time of year," she says on the phone. "Budgets and all, you know."

Dolly doesn't know a lot about state government, but she's pretty sure the fiscal year started in October. She doesn't mind, though; she likes having the apartment to herself. If she gets lonely, she can sit in the dining room and watch the mirror-image family. The baby is learning to walk, and is forever tottering through the room, often crashing head first into a table leg, or tripping on the rug and falling on its nose.

Vishnu's workload at St. J's has gotten very heavy, and his calls are rare, but he'll usually answer if she calls there and has him paged. "Some southern suburbs are very rich," he says, "but I think I will have a practice in Skokie, or Highland Park. It is more select."

"I thought you were going into Emergency Medicine," Dolly says.

"It is best to be self-employed," he says. "Then I can give my own shots."

"Call," she says.

"Dolly, I am often busy," he says patiently.

"No, *call* your own shots," she says.

"Of course!" He laughs heartily. "Oh, this American English! It sets such traps!"

They hang up, and she thinks, Of course, the rich are also the children of God.

Vishnu manages to meet her in a restaurant in Greektown on Valentine's Day. They are seated in the back, near the kitchen, which pleases Dolly; she likes to see the food go by, likes to see the handsome Greek men, muscles bulging, rush past with huge, overloaded trays, the odors of lamb and onions and cinnamon and cardamom dropping from them. Every few minutes, somewhere in the crowded dining room a cheese bursts into flame, and the nearby waiters cry, "O-pah!"

Vishnu has brought her a box of chocolates. "The holiday of love!" he says, beaming at her. She orders a lamb and eggplant stew, and Vishnu orders a goat's head. "Delicious!" he says, tearing apart the skull with his knife and fork. He pokes his fork at her with a grayish lump of animal matter on the tines. "Taste!"

She does taste, and is pleasantly surprised. "Not bad," she says, but she's glad she stuck with a known entity.

They're halfway through the meal when the restaurant's owner rushes from the kitchen to the front door and opens it wide. Even in the back they can feel the cold air sweep the room. Everyone has turned and is staring at the door as three big black men in sunglasses come in, stopping just inside to gaze slowly around the room. Then they step aside, and through the door comes a stunning woman, her light tan skin clear, her hair in a cloud standing out a foot around her head. She wears a white fur hugged up around her neck, and white leather pants, and tall white boots. Behind her is a huge black man, as beautiful as she is, a high color in his shining cheeks, his eyes gleaming as he smiles and shakes hands with the owner. In his arms he carries a tiny, beautiful girl, dressed in white and clutching a toy polar bear.

"Muhammad Ali!" Dolly whispers.

Vishnu nods, and eats more of his goat head.

Muhammad Ali and his entourage—woman, child, bodyguards, and the friends who flow in behind them—move across to the far side of the room, where waiters are frantically shoving tables together to make room for them. All eyes are on Muhammad Ali; no one in the restaurant is eating, except Vishnu. Only after Muhammad Ali is seated do the rest of them turn back to their food. The waiters are all standing near Muhammad Ali; little cameras have materialized in their hands, and the room flickers with the bursts of flashcubes.

"Isn't he beautiful," Dolly says, and she takes a sip of retsina.

Vishnu nods. "For a large man, he moves with grace."

"Float like a butterfly, sting like a bee," she says.

"The bee, I cannot say," Vishnu says. "But at the Governor's Ball, that is exactly it. Floating like the butterfly with the governor's wife."

Dolly's heart stops beating, and she feels the blood rush out of it and into her ears, where it pounds against her eardrums. Maybe, she thinks, the life of that naked polar bear wouldn't be so bad.

She pictures herself naked in the polar bear's pool, slipping from the artificial rocks into the cold green water, diving down to the bottom of the tank, where people are standing with their faces squashed against the viewing window, trying to get a glimpse of her. She swims at them, her cheeks puffed out with air, her eyes bulging; she goes at them fast, and they jump back, but she turns just in time and bends her knees, so that her rear end blooms at them, and they see the soles of her feet flatten against the glass as she shoves off toward the surface. Just her head pops out of the water, and she takes a huge, gasping breath, and goes down again. The sound of human voices is just a blurred humming through the water, a thin, meaningless vibration. It might as well be a polar wind.

"Of course," Vishnu says, stabbing at something in the eye socket of the goat's head, "he is a Muslim."

Belle agrees that it's best if she moves out, and she has packed her clothes, her dishes, and her records, and had all her furniture carted away in a truck. It leaves the apartment rather nude; only Dolly's mattress and box springs and the dining room table remain.

As Belle heads for the door, carrying her last box of books,

Dolly watches her from the living room. "I asked you not to ask him," she says. "I *asked* you."

Belle stares back at her. Dolly thinks that behind her forehead, in back of her eyes, is a vast, blank space. "I didn't think you'd mind," Belle says.

"What were you thinking of?" Dolly says. But of course, with such an empty brain, Belle is incapable of thought.

"Well, if it's any satisfaction," Belle says, with a little laugh, "it wasn't very satisfactory. We didn't hit it off."

"I can't imagine it," Jimmy says. "Did they really sleep together?"

"I don't know," Dolly says. "Also, I don't really want to know."

"Oh, Dolly," Jimmy says, and he shakes his head, as if she's a sad, sad case. "Suppose the Governor's Ball had never occurred. How would your life be different?"

"I would be happy," Dolly says.

"Nonsense," Jimmy says.

"Or suppose she had asked him, but he said no?" Dolly says. "*Then* I would be happy."

"Or suppose things were just the same as they are now, but you never found out?" Jimmy lifts his hands to heaven. "A tree falling in the forest."

"All I know is," Dolly says, and she takes a bite of Twinkie, "I am the fat uncle."

The bus jerks to a stop and they shove their way out. They are at the edge of the river, and they walk out on the bridge and peer over the railing. The river is bright kelly green. Most of the ice chunks still floating in it are white, but a few have sucked up some of the dye and are pale green at the edges, as if they're growing a crop of algae.

They trudge through the crowd, looking for an opening they can seize to watch the parade. There are no gaps; the people in front do not want to budge.

"Dolly! Up here!" Jimmy has scrambled up on top of an electrical substation. He reaches a hand down to her, and in two giant steps she is up beside him.

"Terrific view," she says, and it is. A high school band is marching down the street toward them, playing "Danny Boy." Behind the band is a TV weatherman, who is this year's grand marshall. He marches along in a green velvet cape trimmed with white fur, and a green top hat. Behind him a dozen majorettes in green boots kick down the street, their thighs flashing under their little green skirts. Clowns with green noses zip past on scooters. Shamrock-covered floats move by, bearing Irish queens sitting on papier-mâché Blarney stones. The mayor appears in a green top hat and a green bulletproof vest, surrounded by bodyguards in green bowlers. The mayor is tossing out pieces of green saltwater taffy.

Directly behind him comes a contingent of nurses and residents from St. J.'s, marching along in green surgical scrubs with their stethoscopes swinging from their necks. Vishnu is among them. He waves vigorously, and shouts something to Dolly.

"What?" she shouts back, but he is already past her.

Did he call, "I am loving you"?

Probably not, she thinks, and she sighs. More likely he shouted, "I am a leprechaun."

Jimmy is going to drink green beer at Mrs. O'Leary's Pub, but Dolly's had enough. It's begun to drizzle, and she's cold. She goes down under the street and waits with a thousand other people for the next train. When it comes, it slides to a stop in front of them, but the doors don't open. The lights inside it are out, and she sees her reflection in the window, a little warped and wavery, her eyes big dark hollows under her green ski cap.

Then the lights in the train go on, and the doors slide open. The car is packed. She steps back, but a man reaches out and grabs her hand, and she is hauled in. "The more the merrier," he says.

The train starts with a jerk, and they are whisked northward. Someone has produced a bottle of whiskey, and he is sharing it with the other passengers. Dolly takes a sip; she's never drunk straight whiskey before, and it stings her lips, and feels like lye passing down her throat. She chokes, and coughs, and a woman in a green leopard-skin coat slaps her on the back. She passes the bottle to the man beside her.

"You letting niggers drink your whiskey?" says a voice.

"Be cool, man," says the drinker. "My granddaddy from County Cork."

"Hey, so's mine!" someone says. A man with long dark braids shoves through the crowd and throws his arm across the black man's shoulders. "We could be fucking cousins." He takes a slug of whiskey, and everyone begins to sing, "When Irish Eyes Are Smilin'," though it is clear that nobody knows the words.

The train comes up out of the tunnel and rises past the grimy, blackened bricks of burned-out apartment houses. Now they are elevated, above the streets and cars, and Dolly can just see, now and then, flashes of the lake far to the east. The train swings around a curve, and the passengers in the cars ahead of them wave. Everyone in Dolly's car waves back. The sun comes out.

The train picks up speed, and as they pass Dolly's stop she realizes that they're on the express to the northern suburbs. Someone in the front of the car is throwing up. They've come to Dolly's block now, and they pass her apartment building. She sees her back steps. Next door, the mirror-image family is standing on their back stoop. They wave as the train roars past.

They pass a hospital, and a church, and hundreds of apartment buildings. They flash past an empty train heading south. They whip by platforms where cold people dressed in green are waiting for the local; they rush by a cemetery, where many of the graves have shamrocks on sticks flapping above them in the wind. As she watches the world through the window, her fellow travelers lean against each other, humming and swaying with the motion of the train.

It's like being in *love*, Dolly thinks; and as the train roars on north, into a part of the world where Dolly has never been, she begins to hum along.

Doolittle's Utopia

◆

DOOLITTLE stays away on butchering days. She knows the schedule. Other times she drops in when she's passing by, or goes over when Vita and Rogene are at work. She likes to walk around in the deer pasture, all those little creatures hopping around her. Makes her feel like Snow White.

This has gone on for a long time. Doolittle retired a couple of years ago—a little early, because of her inheritance. She doesn't have a lot of money but she owns her house free and clear, Rogene's son manages her woodlot, and she was employed for nearly forty years, which she figures is long enough. She didn't mind working but she likes not working better.

The deer are Japanese dwarf deer, and Vita and Rogene raise them for the meat. Vita doesn't suffer from anthropomorphism the way Doolittle does. Vita is, as far as Doolittle can tell, without sentimentality. She does what needs to be done and is happy. She has no spare time; all her time is primary, her attention riveted on the task at hand.

Doolittle's time is all spare. She drifts through life. Not to imply that she's unhappy; on the contrary. In a contest of happiness, Doolittle might come out ahead.

Of course, Vita has Rogene. Vita and Rogene, who sells real estate part-time, raised Rogene's two boys, and are partners in the farm. Doolittle thinks it would have been nice to have someone—just someone to sit with when she came home from work for thirty years. If she had had someone to focus her sentiment on, she might be able to butcher deer herself. Instead of vesting them with powers better allowed to a person of her own species: affection, sympathy, fear. When she walks in the deer pasture the little deer talk to her, tell her things by the way they graze, beg for help by nuzzling her ankles. There's nothing she can do to help them. She has no trouble eating them once they've been made into stew.

Today when she drives into the yard Vita's holding a new fawn. "This one's a bruiser," she says. "Next year's alpha buck, I betcha."

Doolittle holds out her arms and Vita pours the little fawn into them, no bigger than a kitten. Doolittle could crush him with a sneeze. The fawn is still. Doolittle can tell by the way he holds his ears that he's pleading with her.

It'll be all right, she says silently. Don't worry. When death comes to the deer, she thinks, they may not know. She read somewhere that animals raised for butchering lack a fear of death. She read that so long ago that she knows it's true.

The white deer walks into Doolittle's yard and pretends to be invisible under the birdfeeder. Her dark eyes stare in Doolittle's window; Doolittle stares back. The white-rumped yearling comes out of the woods, only half mysterious, its unknown father a plain brown deer.

They drift toward the garden, pretending not to know someone is in the house. The white deer leans over the field fence and tears off some lettuce leaves. Doolittle is torn, too: she loves her garden, but having the white deer in her yard is something else.

It is high summer, the air a steady drone of bees, offshore motors, mosquitoes. Doolittle and Rogene and Vita sit on the widow's walk, drinking beer as the sun drops. The widow's walk is the one point on the farm where they can see the ocean; Vita built it after she and Rogene moved in.

Doolittle watches the water through her binoculars. It's calm, smooth: deceptive. She thinks she can see seals drifting with the tide, staring back at her.

One of Rogene's clients has made an offer on a house. "I feel like sending her an anonymous letter," Rogene says. " 'Don't do it! It's a mistake!' "

"Why is she even considering it?" Vita says.

"She has no brain," Doolittle says.

"She's young," Rogene says. "It's her first house. And the house is darling."

"Gets undarling pretty fast when the well runs dry," Vita says.

"I suggested she talk to the women next door," Rogene says. "All the trouble they've had. That should put her off."

"Why can't you just say something?" Doolittle says. "Tell her she's a fool."

Rogene sighs. "You can tell them just so much. Give them information. But you can't tell them not to buy."

"Where is purity?" Doolittle says. "Where is truth, beauty? Sacrificed to the American Way." She drains her beer.

"Doolittle waxes ethical," Vita says. "No death, no injustice, no real estate. Doolittle's Utopia."

It's true: Doolittle despises real estate agents, insurance agents, and the owners of yachts over thirty-two feet long. Unless she knows them personally, anyway. She gets along fine with Fred Hamblen, her Allstate agent. And of course there's Rogene.

Doolittle reaches for another beer and pops the tab.

"Destry's coming down next week," Rogene says.

"Hey, Doo." Sure enough, Destry has come with her firewood. Doolittle comes out of the woods. Destry has backed the truck across the yard and is unhooking the back panel. "What's up, Doolittle?" he says.

"I'm looking for white deer droppings," Doolittle says.

"The white deer's been around?" Destry says. He looks off into the woods, hoping to see it slip through the trees.

Doolittle comes up close to the truck and breathes deep, taking in beech and maple and oak and Destry. Life is like this: in the middle of summer, a whiff of winter.

"Woodlot's doing good," Destry says. "Warren says he saw an ivorybill in there last month."

"An ivorybill," Doolittle says.

Destry grins. "Said he went home and got his camcorder, but it never came back. He heard it again though. They're shy birds, Doo."

"Warren is some naturalist," Doolittle says.

Destry trips the truck bed back and wood pours out. Doolittle thinks she will never get tired of hearing it thud onto the hard-packed dirt, straight clay under the grass, where she has had it dumped every summer for twenty-four years. Much as seeing Destry reminds her of dying, much as the smell of fresh-cut wood makes her hear it crying out in grief, she still gets excited, still gets her satisfaction from seeing the wood-pile build up again.

"So," Destry says, accepting the beer she offers, "this deer leaves white scat, huh?"

"It wouldn't surprise me," Doolittle says.

Every year she swears it's the last, but she can't bring herself to hire anyone, or to ask Destry to bring the wood already split. Someone with a log splitter could finish off this load in an hour. What are you trying to prove? she snarls at herself; but there's no answer.

She hates the chainsaw. The very word is synonymous in her mind with losing-a-leg. Every time she hauls it out of the shed and starts it up she's filled with visions of it slipping, flipping out of her hands and turning on her, slicing through her femoral artery, whipping off a hand on the rebound. She lies in a pool of blood, a fountain of blood, in her own yard, among her own goddamned logs. No one happens by. Her blood shoots out of her in seconds; no one could help anyway; she's dead in the sun, and when the chainsaw finally runs out of gas there is silence for a few moments before the birds start up again.

Sometimes she lies there for days before anyone finds her. Once in a while someone comes in time to say good-bye: Vita, or Destry, or, if she's feeling very sorry for herself, Rogene.

She pulls the starter cord and the chainsaw jumps into life. Oh, but she loves it, the power it has, the power she has when it's in her arms. The chain slipping through oak like a spatula through chèvre. Like a feather through a cake-mix cake. Like a knife through the throat of a fawn.

Next time around, Doolittle thinks, nothing's going to scare me.

When Rogene's ready to throw the lobsters into the pots, Doolittle heads for the barn. Even from there she can hear them, their claws scrabbling against the lid, their sharp lobster-cries slipping out of the pots in the steam. Doolittle hums a little, and talks to the dwarf deer. They come to the edges of their pens and suck on her fingers, and she has to apologize for being dry, empty, nobody's mother.

"Doolittle! You can come back now!" Vita's waving from up in the yard where the tables are set up. It's the annual lobster feed, Rogene's boys down, family and pseudo-family gathered. Doolittle is the pseudo-family—she invented the term for herself. Somebody who's always there, but wouldn't be notified if someone in the real family died. For a long time she carried a list of people to notify in case she died. But she doesn't have it any more.

Small brought a girl with him. Every time one of the boys

brings a girl down, Rogene flaps around for days. But they never stick—the boys seem unable to mate, or breed. This girl, Lisa, is dark haired and has bad skin. If she would only smile, Doolittle thinks, we'd see a broken tooth, and that would be the end of it. But the girl hardly opens her mouth. She's nervous and silent, maybe even a teenager.

"Doo's got the white deer on her property," Destry says.

"Everyone's got the white deer these days," Rogene says. "Vita thinks there's more than one."

"A herd of white deer," Small says. "There's a tourist attraction for you, Ma."

"White deer?" says Lisa.

"More corn, anyone?" Rogene says.

"Probably ghost deer," Doolittle says. "There's no scientific explanation."

"All come back to haunt Vita," Destry says.

Lisa's full of surprises. "You mean albino, right?"

"No, that's different," Vita says. "Albinos lack pigmentation. These are from a closed population, with a dominant white spotting gene."

Destry takes an ear of corn from the bowl Rogene's holding beside his head. "Vita, we're talking deer here, not pigs," he says.

Doolittle passes him the butter. "Deer, Vita, not fashion." She leans over to look at the discarded lobster shells in the middle of the table. "Waste," she says. She sucks the meat out of a tiny leg, then picks up a carapace and scrapes out the fat and tomalley with her finger. She sucks it off loudly. "Sin," she says, staring at Lisa, "is wasting this stuff."

"Big white lobsters come and get you," Small says.

Lisa smiles. A canine is missing.

Rogene smiles. "Lisa, honey, more corn?" she says.

Doolittle drifts through the woods. You'd think by now she'd know her way around, and in a way she does. She knows every inch of these woods, is on good terms with the mosses, the ferns, the mushroom patches. She doesn't get lost; it's just that she never quite knows where she'll come out.

This is the first summer in forty years she's been without a dog. Vita put Wiggins down last fall, after he'd gotten so thin, because he was dreading winter. Now Doolittle edges through the woods alone and never knows what the crashing in the underbrush might be. Deer, or black bears—there are known dens on the island—or a stray moose, or a bobcat. Doolittle would like to see any of them.

She thought she'd always want dogs, but the calculations have changed. A dog's life could be longer than hers, and would that be fair? Besides, things have happened since Wiggins went that never happened before. The white deer eating her lettuce, for one thing. And one night she heard the coyotes closer than ever, and she looked out her bedroom window to see three of them trotting up her driveway. They stopped near the car and sang some more, and then one stood on three legs and scratched her head with the fourth, while another lifted his leg against a tire. He moved slowly around the yard as the others watched and yawned, marking all the spots where Wiggins's messages had begun to fade. Then they all turned and went back down the drive.

Wiggins always demanded motion, too. More and more now Doolittle just stops, stands next to a tree or sits down on a glacial erratic. She has no territory she needs to cover. Now shrews peer at her from under the dead oak leaves, and porkies inch their way down tree trunks and amble off, paying no attention to her. This is very satisfying, almost as if she isn't even there.

She's near the shore now, in someone's private woods. She can hear the chunking of engines—people checking their traps. She follows the sound, and others chime in: gulls, a bell buoy, more engines. The trees have thinned, and Doolittle sees the ocean glinting through them. She comes out on

Turnbull Head, forty feet above the water. The shore is all granite here, ledge jutting out over a strip of popplestone beach. It is a beautiful day, sunny, warm, and if Doolittle had brought her field glasses she could see the cows on the island across the strait.

The white deer is on a ledge below her, ten or more feet above the water. She is half standing, her front feet slipping in the rockweed as she works to pull up her hindquarters. One haunch rests in a tidepool, the hind legs sticking out at a bad angle. Now and then a front hoof clacks on the rock, or slips with a shoosh through the wet vegetation. Doolittle, thirty feet above, can see a dullness in her eye, a lack of pleading, the doe empty of anything but the rote struggle to stand.

Three lobster boats drum as gently as they can in the deep water beneath the deer's ledge, the lobstermen smoking, stroking the levers and pulleys soothingly, watching the white deer. A Coast Guard Zodiac chugs around the point and in under the ledge. It is the usual thing, the little boat jockeying in the waves, men shouting, men in frogsuits leaping overboard and wading onto the narrow beach, running back and forth looking for a path up the cliff. No path. Hours pass, and the white deer scrabbles on the wet rocks. The tide is either coming in or going out.

The sky throbs and out of the trees above Doolittle's head comes the Search and Rescue helicopter. It swings down toward the water and dangles a rope ladder above the frogmen on the beach. One grabs it and the helicopter lifts him into the air, then drops him on the ledge with the deer. He waits until the helicopter fetches another frogman, and together they approach the deer.

She stops moving, and the men lay hands on her, one stroking her neck heavily and the other moving his hands down her ribs. The men are shaking their heads, and the white deer's eye is looking straight up at Doolittle. It'll be all right, Doolittle tells the deer, you'll be all right. Under the roar of the helicopter, the thrumming of the lobster boats, the screaming gulls and the waves and the wind that's started up in the cedars, Doolittle hears the men murmuring to the deer, and the chuffing of the deer's breath, and the beating of her own heart, the blood in her ears.

It'll be all right, she says. The helicopter moves in close again, and the men fasten something, a sling, around the deer, hooking it under her chest and strapping it between her back legs, testing the rope that attaches the sling to the helicopter. The helicopter moves skyward and the deer is jerked into the air, legs and head swinging, in a motion that must give excruciating pain to a deer with a broken back. But Doolittle knows the deer is beyond pain, has in fact felt no pain since death became certain, is as good as dead now. The deer rises nearly to where Doolittle stands before the helicopter turns to head for the low land around the point. Doolittle looks up and there is Vita's face framed in the Plexiglas bubble; it is Vita at the controls.

The lobstermen turn their boats out into the strait and head out, throttles wide. The sound of the helicopter is suddenly soft as it goes around the headland. Below Doolittle the frogmen lean back on their hands on White Deer Ledge and hold their faces up to the sun, waiting for rescue.

Destry's down for the Winter Carnival, and Doolittle's waiting for him in the woods. She stands in the snow a few feet off the trail, in a piece of sunlight. If he doesn't show up soon she'll empty the flask of lemon vodka by herself.

A chickadee drops onto a branch and cocks its head at her. "Waiting for Destry," she says, and it zips off, satisfied.

She hears him coming, screaming through the woods, and she steps out of the trees to the edge of the path. He's in Day-Glo orange, and his Ski-Doo is fire engine red. It slides to a stop inches from her shins.

"Woman of my dreams," Destry says, and she hands him

the flask. His teeth flash in his forest of beard. His eyes are gone, hidden in goggles.

Doolittle climbs on and settles herself behind him, snugging her thighs up against his and sliding her hands in their buckskin mittens around his ribs. The first time she saw him his stomach was much the same, a good proportion of his body, but it was full of milk then, and strained peas. Now it's beer.

"Ready?" Destry shouts.

"Ready," she shouts back.

He kicks the Ski-Doo into action and it leaps down the trail. "Hoo-oo!" he screams. "Destry rides again!"

It's what he yells every time. It kicks his vision of himself into gear, Doolittle thinks. At his first Winter Carnival he sat in front of her, in a similar snowsuit, on a big old inner tube, and when she kicked them off at the top of the ice slide he screamed the same thing.

They've taken this ride before. Doolittle knows everything about it, the way the wind will shred the top layer of skin on her face, the way his body feels through six or eight layers of cloth, the drops and bursts of her heart as they lean into curves, swerve into snowbanks to avoid bewildered squirrels. She will be deaf and in pain and frozen for hours afterwards, and so will he. They will hardly be able to move, be unable to think, will chock up the stove and fall asleep in its heavy heat.

Doolittle hates these machines, hates the sound of them, the idea of them, the speed with which they shoot through the forest careless of anything. Every time, it shocks her that she's clinging to a man who could have been anything, a lawyer, a dancer, a professor of English, but who instead went feral, turned away from a certain light and now just stumps through the woods into middle age. She can't see what she means: he hunts, he'd rather drink than think, he's hoping to win the lottery. Yet he knows the truth about ivorybills.

She can't let go.

Margaret Mead

◆

MY FATHER called at noon to say he was bringing Margaret Mead and Professor Curtis, one of the bachelors, home for dinner before the lecture.

"Wonderful," my mother said into the telephone. "What am I supposed to serve, roast boar?"

"Mangoes," Auntie Roxie said. "Then we can all sit on the kitchen floor and talk about menstruation taboos."

My mother hung up and went out to the kitchen to make a batch of Bloody Marys. We followed her.

"Seriously," Auntie Roxie said. "What are you going to serve?"

"Indigenous American food," my mother said. "Hot dogs."

Auntie Roxie was looking through the cupboards. "Here we go. B&M baked beans."

"Do you think I've got time for jello salad?" my mother said.

"With miniature marshmallows!" Jane said.

"And maraschino cherries," I said.

"When a famous chieftain from the South Seas comes, the women gather in the kitchen to prepare food," Auntie Roxie said in a deep voice. "Even the prepubescent girl children help."

"Do you think she'll get it?" said my mother, getting a package of hot dogs out of the freezer.

"She's an intellectual, isn't she?" said Auntie Roxie.

"What is Margaret Mead a chief of?" I asked Jane.

"I cannot believe how dumb you are," she said. "You are so stupid you don't even know about Margaret Mead."

"Yes I do," I said. "But I thought she was a poet."

"I'm not supposed to tell you this," Jane said, looking up from painting her fingernails, "but you were a blue baby."

"I know that," I said. "Think of another one, dumbbell." I watched her coat her nails with scarlet polish. "Mom's going to be mad."

"No she's not," Jane said. "She said I should do this for Margaret Mead. Here." She motioned me closer with the little brush. "I'll do yours, too."

I sat outside to wait. Mr. Curtis was the first to arrive, his camera around his neck as usual. "Hi, Charlotte," he shouted. "Are you ready to marry me yet?"

Mr. Curtis was forever asking me to marry him. I was terrified at the prospect. "I'm not old enough," I said.

He loomed over me. "We could have a betrothal ceremony," he said. "In Samoa girls get betrothed when they're eight years old."

"I'm only seven," I whispered.

"Sometimes they're seven," he said. "To celebrate our betrothal, I'll take your picture. Say litchi nut."

I tried to smile.

He lowered the camera. "Well," he said. "How about just a natural shot. Try to look natural."

I tried to relax.

"Jesus," said Mr. Curtis. "You look like a mongoloid idiot." He put the cover back on his camera. "Where is your beautiful mother?" He leaped up the steps and in the front door.

Margaret Mead was a short lady wearing a jacket like my father's and a skirt that came below her knees. My father rushed around to open her door for her and help her out of the car. As they came up the walk, laughing, I strolled away toward the grape arbor. I had been hoping for feathers, but she was wearing glasses.

I lay down under the vines and gazed at my blood-red nails as I picked grapes from the bunches that dangled near me. The scarlet fingernails looked beautiful against the deep purple of the Concord grapes; slowly my fingertips too turned purple. I waved my hands exotically above my face and hummed.

"I suppose you're being a hula dancer," Jane said.

"None of your beeswax," I said, and got up. "Are they eating yet? Did she get it?"

"She's an intellectual, isn't she?" Jane said. "Anyway, no. They're still having cocktails. Daddy said we should come and meet her."

"She looks like a turtle," I said.

We went in through the kitchen, where my mother and Auntie Roxie were both leaning against the sink smoking. My mother waved us toward the door. "Go on in," she said. "Be presented to the royalty."

Margaret Mead was sitting in the green upholstered chair in the corner of the living room. Jane stopped at the door, and I bumped into her. My father put down his glass and beckoned us in. "Girls," he said, "I'd like you to meet Margaret Mead. She's a very famous anthropologist. My daughters, Jane and Charlotte."

We stood and looked at her, and she looked at us from behind her glasses. "How nice to meet you," Margaret Mead said.

Jane sat down on the sofa. "I hope you're enjoying your visit to our country, Mrs. Mead," she said politely.

"You can sit on the floor if you want to," I said.

"Thank you, I'm quite comfortable," she said. "What lovely fingernails you have."

"Yes, it's what prepubescent girls do when a chieftain comes," Jane said.

I held out my grape-stained hands. "Do they do this in Samoa?"

"As a matter of fact," Margaret Mead said, "they do something very much like that."

"I hope you enjoy our meal," Jane said. "We helped with it."

"Jello salad!" I said. "With marshmallows."

"My," said Margaret Mead.

"Excuse me," my father said. "I'll just check on dinner." He headed out the door toward the kitchen.

"Do you know Eleanor Roosevelt?" Jane said.

"We're acquainted, yes," said Margaret Mead. "She's an admirable woman."

Conversation flagged. Mr. Curtis gazed out the window, and Margaret Mead sat looking at us. Jane gave me a worried look. She hated silences.

In desperation, I said, "Would you like to see us dance?"

Margaret Mead sat back in the green chair and clasped her hands in her lap. "I'd like that very much," she said.

Jane rolled her eyes, and said to Margaret Mead, "I'm too old for dancing, but Charlotte's very good at it. She was practicing out in the grape arbor."

"Well then, Charlotte, I'd like to see you dance," Margaret Mead said.

"Is this a wedding dance?" Mr. Curtis said, and he winked at me.

"No," I said. "This is a menstruation dance, from the South Seas." I positioned myself in the middle of the room, gave Jane a dirty look, and slowly began to dance, waving my arms and weaving my hips. "A-lo-ha hooey," I sang, just as our Brownie troop had sung last spring for the Vercingetorix School Fish Fry. "A-lo-ha hooey."

Mr. Curtis jumped around taking pictures of me. Jane drummed her fingers on the arm of the sofa. Margaret Mead never took her eyes off me.

She seemed so interested I finally said, "Would you like me to teach you?"

Margaret Mead was taken by surprise. Then she smiled. "I'd love that," she said.

She stood beside me in the middle of the rug, and I showed her how to hold her arms. "Just step back and forth," I said. "Step, touch. Step, touch." She was a quick study. By the third time through, she had the steps down pat, and she knew the words.

"A-lo-ha hooey," we sang.

After a while Jane got up to dance too, and finally Mr. Curtis stopped taking pictures and got in line beside Margaret Mead. I showed them how to hold their elbows and make their hands wave like palm trees. We swayed toward the door and into the dining room, and we danced around the table, singing.

"I hope you like good old beans and franks, Margaret," said my mother, bringing a casserole in and setting it on the table.

Margaret Mead plopped down in her chair and beamed at my mother. "And jello salad?" she said. "My favorite meal."

Before she left for the lecture that evening, she came over to say good-bye to me and Jane. "I had such a nice time," she said. We shook her hand.

"I hope you enjoy the lecture," Jane said.

"Well, I'm giving it," said Margaret Mead. "I think it's pretty good."

I followed her toward the door. "Mrs. Mead!" I whispered. "I hope you don't think I'm a mongoloid idiot."

"Good lord!" she said. "It never crossed my mind."

"You don't even know what that means," Jane said when we went upstairs.

"I do too," I said. "Don't you?"

Jane was applying polish to her toenails. "We should have done our toes, too," she said. "It would have been more realistic."

I took off my socks and sat down beside her, waiting for her to finish her toes and do mine.

"I know what an idiot is," Jane said, "but I'm not too sure about mongoloid."

"Me neither," I said.

"You have really ugly toes," she said.

I looked at them sadly. "I know it," I said.

I forgot the visit of Margaret Mead for over thirty years, until a day when Jane and I were cleaning out my parents' basement after my mother died. I opened an old photo album, and when I found a picture of myself, fingernails painted, sitting expressionlessly on the front steps, the day came flooding back.

Jane didn't remember any of it. "Our mother would never have served hot dogs to Margaret Mead," she said.

I showed her the album.

"Where are the ones of you and Margaret Mead doing the hula?" she said.

It was true, there were no pictures of Margaret Mead and me—and Jane—dancing in the living room; and I couldn't ask my parents or Professor Curtis about it, because they are all dead.

Jane and I each took what we wanted from our parents' house and gave the rest to Goodwill.

"Why are you keeping that thing?" she said, when I took the old green chair.

"Because Margaret Mead sat there," I started to say; but instead I said, "I just sort of like it," which is just as true.

Better Be Ready
'Bout Half Past Eight

◆

"**I**'M changing sex," Zach said.

Byron looked up from his lab notebook. "For the better, I hope."

"This is something I've never discussed with you," Zach said, stepping back and leaning against the cold-room door. "I need to. Do you want to go get a beer or something?"

"I have to transcribe this data," Byron said. "What do you need to discuss?"

"My sexuality," Zach said. "The way I feel trapped in the wrong body."

"Well, I suppose you were right," Byron said.

"Right?" Zach said.

"Not to discuss it with me," Byron said. "It's none of my business, is it?"

"We've been friends a long time," Zach said.

"Have you always felt this way?" Byron said.

Zach nodded. "I didn't know it was this I was feeling," he said. "But I've been in therapy for over a year now, and I'm sure."

"You've been seeing Terry about *this*?" Byron had given Zach the name of Terry Wu, whom he himself had once consulted professionally.

Zach nodded again. "He's terrific. He knew the first time he met me what I was."

"What were you?" Byron said.

"A woman," Zach said.

Had there been any signs? Frowning, Byron sat staring at the computer screen. Then he stood, shoved his hands into his pockets, and stared out the window. He could see the sky and the top of the snow-covered hills. On this floor all the windows started at chin level, so you couldn't see the parking lot or the ground outside; you could only see distances, clouds, and sections of sunrise.

He walked up and down the hall for a while. The surrounding labs buzzed with action, students leaning intently over whirring equipment, technicians laughing over coffee. Secretaries clopped through the hall and said, "Hi, Dr. Glass" when they passed him. He could ignore them because he had a reputation for being absentminded; he was absorbed in his research, or perhaps in a new poem. He was well known, particularly in scientific circles, for his poetry. He edited the poetry column of *Science*. He judged many poetry-writing competitions, and he had edited anthologies.

What had he missed?

Worrying about it was useless. Zach's life wasn't *his* concern. "Just as long as it doesn't interfere with work," he would say. "I can't have personal life running amok in the lab."

But in fact he didn't believe in the separation of work and home. "If your love life's screwed up, you're probably going to screw up the science," he'd said more than once when he sent a sobbing technician home, or gave a distraught graduate student the name of a counselor. As a result his workers did sacrifice, to some extent, their personal lives to come in on weekends or at night to see to an experiment. It worked out.

"Go on home," he imagined himself saying to Zach, patting him on the shoulder. "Come back when it's all over."

But that wouldn't work. For one thing, it wouldn't end. For another thing, Zach wouldn't be Zach when he came back. He would be a woman Byron had never met.

"He's putting you on," Emily said. She was sitting at the table, ostensibly editing a paper on the synthesis of mRNA at the transcriptional level in the Drosophila per protein; but whenever the spoon Byron held approached Toby's open mouth, her own mouth opened in anticipation.

"Nope," Byron said, spooning more applesauce from the jar. "He wanted to tell me before he started wearing makeup."

"If Zach thinks that's the definition of women, he's headed for trouble," Emily said. "I suppose he's shaving his legs and getting silicone implants, too."

"Not to mention waxing his bikini line," Byron said.

"Oh, God," Emily said, laughing. "I don't want to hear any more." She handed Byron a washcloth, and Byron carefully wiped applesauce off Toby's chin. "How would you know you were the wrong sex?"

"Woman's intuition?" Byron said.

"Very attractive," he said the next morning, when Zach walked into the lab wearing eye shadow.

"Don't make fun of me, okay?" Zach said.

Byron felt embarrassed. "I didn't mean anything," he said. "I mean, it's subtle, and everything."

Zach looked pleased. "I've been practicing," he said. "You know what? My younger brother wears more makeup than I do. Is this a crazy world or what?"

"Yeah," Byron said. He'd met Zach's brother, whose makeup was usually black. "Are you doing this gradually? Or are you sort of going cold turkey? I mean, will you come in in nylons and spike heels some morning?"

"Babe," Zach said, "I've been getting hormones for six months. Don't you notice anything different?"

He put his hands on his hips and turned slowly around, and Byron saw discernible breasts pushing up the cloth of Zach's rugby shirt. Byron felt a little faint, but he managed to say, "You're wearing a bra."

Zach went over to look in the mirror behind the door. He stood on tiptoe, staring intently at his breasts for a moment, and then, as he took his lab coat off the hook, he said, "God, I'm starting to feel good."

"You are?" was all Byron could manage. He was wondering how to say, without hurting Zach's new feelings, Don't call me Babe.

All day he tried not to look at Zach's breasts, but there they were, right in front of him, as Zach bent over the bench, or peered into the microscope, or leaned back with his hands behind his neck, staring at the ceiling, thinking.

"I'm heading out," Byron told Sarah in midafternoon.

"Are you okay?" she said, looking up from the bench. "You look a little peaked."

"I'm fine," Byron said. "I'll be back in the morning."

But once out in the parking lot, sitting in his car, he could think of no place he wanted to go. He hung on to the steering wheel and stared at the Mercedes in front of him, which had a Utah license plate that read IMAQT. A woman, of course.

Well, it's not *my* life, he thought. Nothing has changed for me.

"I haven't had this much trouble with breasts since I was sixteen," he said to Emily as they sat at the kitchen table watching the sunset.

"How big are they?" Emily said.

"Jesus, I don't know," Byron said.

"Bigger than mine?" she said.

Byron looked at Emily's breasts, which were bigger since she'd had Toby. "No," he said. "But I think they've just started."

"You mean he'll just keep taking hormones till they're the size he wants?" Emily said. "I should do that."

"You know," Byron said, "what I don't understand is why it bothers me so much. You'd think he's doing it to spite me."

"Going to meetings will be more expensive," she said.

"What do you mean?" Byron said.

"Honey," Emily said, "if Zach's a woman, you won't be sharing a room. Will you?"

"Oh," Byron said. "Do you think it will make that much difference?"

"You're already obsessed with his breasts," Emily said. "Wait till he's fully equipped."

Byron leaned his head on his hand. He hadn't even *thought* about the surgical procedure.

"I think you're letting this come between us," Zach said the next day.

"What?" Byron said.

"We've been friends a long time. I don't want to lose that."

"Zach," Byron said, "I don't see how things can stay the same."

"But I'm still the same person," Zach said.

Byron was not at all sure of that. "Well, how's it going?" he finally said.

Zach seemed pleased to be asked. He sat down on the desk and folded his arms. "Really well," he said. "The surgeon says the physiological changes are right on schedule. I'm scheduled for surgery starting next month."

"Starting?" Byron said.

"It's a series of operations," Zach said. "Probably about six, over a couple of months. Cosmetic surgery for the most part."

"Zach," Byron said, "maybe it's none of my business, but don't you feel"—he cast about for the right way to say it— "doesn't it make you feel mutilated?"

Zach shook his head. "That's what it's all about," he said. "It *doesn't*. To tell you the truth, in the last year or two I've come to feel as if my penis is an alien growth on my body. It's my *enemy*, Byron. This surgery's going to liberate me."

Byron crossed his legs. "I don't think I can relate to that," he said.

"I know," Zach said. "My support group says nobody really understands."

"Your support group?"

"Women who've had the operation," Zach said, "or are in the process. We meet every week."

"How many are there?" Byron said.

"More than you'd think," Zach said.

"So," Byron said. "Are you—I mean, should I call you 'she' now?"

Zach grinned. "I've been calling myself 'she' for a while. But so far nobody outside my group has."

"Well," Byron said. He tried to look at Zach and smile, but he couldn't do both at once. He smiled first, and then looked. "I'll work on it," he said. "But it's not exactly easy for me either, you know."

"I know. I really appreciate your trying to understand." Zach stood up. "Back to work," he said. "Oh." He turned around with his hand on the doorknob. "I'm changing my name, too. As of next month, I'll be Zoe."

"Zoe," Byron said.

"It means 'life,'" Zach said. "Mine is finally beginning."

"It means 'life,'" Byron said mincingly to Toby as he pulled the soggy diaper out from under him. "Life, for Christ's sake."

Toby smiled.

"What's he been for thirty-eight years—dead?" Byron said. He dried Toby and sprinkled him with powder, smoothing it into the soft creases. As he lifted Toby's feet to slide a clean diaper underneath him, a stream of pee arced gracefully into the air and hit Byron in the chest, leaving a trail of droplets across Toby's powdered thighs.

"Oh, geez," Byron said. "Couldn't you wait ten seconds?" He reached for the washcloth and wiped the baby off. Then he wiggled the little penis between his thumb and forefinger. "You know what you are, don't you?" he said, leaning over and peering into Toby's face. "A little man. No question about that."

Toby laughed.

After he'd put Toby into the crib, Byron went into the bathroom, pulling his T-shirt off. He caught sight of himself in the mirror and stood still. With the neckband of the shirt stuck on his head, framing his face, the shirt hung from his head like a wig of green hair.

He took his glasses off to blur the details and moved close to the glass, looking at the line of his jaw. Was his jaw strong? Some women who had what were called "strong features" were quite attractive. Byron's mother used to say that Emily was built like a football player, but Byron had always thought she was sexy.

He put his glasses on and stepped back, bending his knees so that only his shoulders showed in the glass. With long hair around his face, and a few hormones to change his shape a little, he'd make a terrific woman.

He opened the medicine cabinet and took out one of Emily's lipsticks. He leaned forward and spread it on his mouth, and as he pressed his lips together, a woman's face materialized in the mirror. Byron's heart came to a standstill.

It was his mother.

"It was the weirdest thing," he said. "I never looked like her before. Never."

"You never cross-dressed before," Zach said, continuing to stare at the video monitor. "What's going on with this data?"

"Of course I never cross-dressed," Byron said. "I still

don't cross-dress. I just happened to look in the mirror when my shirt was on my head."

Zach looked up at him and grinned. "And there she was," he said. "You would be amazed what we find out about ourselves when we come to terms with our sexuality."

"Oh, for God's sake," Byron said. "I was taking my shirt off. I wasn't coming to terms with anything."

"That's fairly obvious," Zach said, tapping at the keyboard.

"Jesus!" Byron said. "Do those hormones come complete with bitchiness? Or is your period starting?"

Zach stared at him. "I can't believe you said that," he said.

Byron couldn't believe he'd said it either, but he went on. "Everything's sexuality with you these days," he said crossly. "I'm trying to tell you about my mother and you tell me it's my goddamn sexuality."

Zach stood up and stepped away from the desk. "Look," he said, folding his arms, "it's called the Tiresias syndrome. You're jealous because I understand both sexes. By cross-dressing—whether you go around in Emily's underwear or just pretend you've got a wig on—you're trying to identify with me."

For a long moment Byron was unable to move. "What?" he finally said.

"You can't handle talking about the things that really matter, can you?" Zach said. "As soon as we get close to personal feelings, you back off."

"Feelings," Byron said.

"You're a typical man when it comes to emotions," Zach said.

"And you're a typical woman," Byron said.

Zach shook his head. "You are in trouble, boy."

"*I'm* in trouble?" Byron said. "Looks to me like you're the one with the problem."

"That's the difference between us," Zach said. "I'm taking steps to correct my problem. You won't even admit yours."

"My problem is you," Byron said. "You are a fucking prick."

"Not for long," Zach said.

"Once a prick, always a prick," Byron shouted.

After Zach walked out the door, Byron sat down at his desk and stared at the data Zach had pulled up on the screen, but its sense eluded him. Finally he spun his chair around and put his feet up on the bookcase behind him, and reached for a legal pad.

He always wrote his poetry on long yellow legal pads. He had once tried to jot down some poetic thoughts on the computer, but they had slipped out of his poem and insinuated themselves into a new idea for a research project, which in fact developed into a grant proposal that was later funded. The experience had scared him.

He stared up at the slice of sky that was visible from where he sat, and held the legal pad on his lap for over an hour, during which he wrote down thirteen words. When Sarah stuck her head into the office and said, "See you tomorrow," he put the pad down and left work for the day.

Driving home he thought about his dead mother, Melba Glass. She had never liked Emily, but once Byron was married, his mother stopped saying snide things about her. She asked them instead. "Honey," she'd say, "isn't Emily a little *strident?*"

"What do you mean, *strident?*" Byron would snarl, and she would say she'd meant nothing at all, really, young women were just *different* these days. Byron would narrow his eyes at her; but later, when he'd driven his mother to the train station and waved her off, the idea would come back to him. Emily *was* vociferous in her opinions. And not particularly tolerant of her mother-in-law's old-fashioned tendencies.

"Why doesn't your mother even fucking *drive?*" she'd say.

"Why should she?" Byron said. "She never needed to."

"She needs to now, doesn't she?" Emily said.

"Why should she?" Byron would repeat; and for a couple of days he would react to everything Emily said as if she was being highly unreasonable, and *strident*.

What would Emily say if he told her that his dead mother had appeared to him? Worse, that he had appeared to himself as his dead mother?

She would lean over Toby's crib in the dark. "I'll be Don Ameche in a taxi, honey," she'd sing. "Better be ready 'bout half past eight."

"How are you? Three of you now. Ha!" Terry Wu said.

"Three of me?" Byron said.

"You have a little baby?" Terry said.

"Oh! Toby! Terrific! And Emily. I see. Sure, we're fine. Really. Everything's terrific."

A concerned look seized Terry Wu's face. "Do you protest too much?" he said, and he leaned forward, pressing his fingertips together.

"Protest?" Byron said. "That's not why I'm here."

"Maybe no, maybe yes," Terry said, but he leaned back again.

"No, it's my, uh, colleague. You know, Zach."

"Ah," Terry said.

"I seem obsessed," Byron said weakly.

"You are obsessed with your colleague?"

"With his sex," Byron said.

"*His* sex?" Terry said.

Byron felt himself blushing. "I can't get used to the idea that he's a woman."

Terry nodded again. "Each one is a mystery."

"No, it's just—why didn't I know?"

"Did you know your wife was pregnant when she conceived?"

"What does that have to do with it?" Byron said.

"Well," Terry said, "you were there when it happened, in fact you did the deed, and yet you didn't know about it."

"Terry, I think that's something else."

Terry shrugged. "Are you in love with your colleague?"

"Of course not." He was getting angry. "What are you getting at?"

"I am trying to elicit a coherent statement from you," Terry said. "So far all you have managed to tell me is that you are obsessed with your colleague and are not in love with her. I am having trouble following your flight of ideas."

"Look." Byron looked down at his feet. "Someone whom I have known for more than twenty years has overnight turned into a woman. It's shaken my understanding of reality. I can no longer trust what I see before my eyes."

"Yet you call yourself a scientist," Terry said thoughtfully. "It is simply a matter of surgery and hormonal therapy, isn't it? Changing one form into another by a well-documented protocol?"

Byron stared at him. "That's not what I mean," he said.

Terry clasped his hands together happily. "Yet there is a magical process involved as well! An invisible and powerful force! Something that is beyond our understanding! But"—he put his hands on his desk and stared into Byron's eyes—"even your poetic license will not allow you to accept it?"

"My poetic license?" Byron said.

"Are man and woman so different, so unrelated, that no transformation is possible? It's this Western culture," Terry said in disgust. "In my country, people exchange sexes every day."

Byron wondered if he had understood Terry correctly.

"Suppose your little baby comes to you in twenty years and says, 'Daddy, I am now Chinese.' Will you disown the child, after twenty years of paternity? No! He will still be the son you love."

"Chinese?" Byron said.

"I fear our time is up," Terry said. He stood up and held his hand out. Byron stood, too, and shook it. "Good to see you again. Would you like to resume these discussions on a regular basis? I can see you at this time every week."

"I don't think so," Byron said. "I just wanted this one consultation."

"Glad to be of service," Terry said. "No charge, no charge. Professional courtesy. Someday I may need an experiment!" He chuckled. "Or a poem."

"A shower?" Byron said.

"Isn't it a kick?" Emily said. "Gifts like garter belts and strawberry douches."

"That's sick," he said.

"Oh, come on, honey. His men friends are invited too." She put down the screwdriver she'd been using to put together Toby's Baby Bouncer and leaned over to kiss Byron's knee. "It'll be fun."

"Why don't we just play Red Rover?" Byron said. "All the girls can stand on one side and yell, 'Let Zach come on over.'"

"You act as if you've lost your best friend," Emily said.

"I *am* losing him. I've known him all these years and suddenly I find out he's the opposite of what I thought he was."

"Ah," Emily said, and she sat back against the sofa. "Here we go. Men and women are diametrically opposed."

"Don't you start," he said. "I don't need an attack on the home front."

"I'm supposed to comfort you, I suppose," Emily said. "Sympathize with you because your good buddy's going over to the enemy."

"Well?" Byron said. "Aren't you secretly glad? Having a celebration? Letting him in on all your girlish secrets?"

Emily shook her head. "We're talking about a human being who has suffered for forty years, and you're jealous because we're giving him some lacy underpants? You're welcome to borrow some of mine, if that's what you want." She smiled at him.

"Suffered?" Byron said. "The dire fate of living in a male body? A fate worse than death, clearly."

"Why are you attacking *me?*" Emily said.

"I'm not attacking you," he said. "I'm just upset." He scooted closer to her and put his arms around her, laying his head against her breasts. "What if I lost you, too?"

"Sweetheart," Emily said, "you're stuck with me for the duration."

"I hope so," Byron said. He turned his head and pressed his face against her. "I certainly hope so." His voice, caught in her cleavage, sounded very far away.

"Many, many years ago," Byron said softly, holding Toby in his arms as he rocked in the dark, "when Daddy and Uncle Zach were very young—"

Toby, who was gazing at his eyes as he spoke, flung out his fist.

"He was still Uncle Zach at the time," Byron said. He tucked the fist into his armpit. "Anyway, we used to ride out to the quarries to go swimming. You've never been swimming, but it's a lot like bobbing around in Mummy's uterus."

Toby's eyes closed.

"We used to ride our bikes out there after we'd finished our lab work," Byron said. "Riding a bike in the summertime in southern Indiana is a lot like swimming. The air is so full of humidity you can hardly push the sweat out your pores.

"So we would ride out there in the late afternoon, and hide our bikes in the trees, and go out to our favorite jumping-off place," Byron said. "And Daddy and Uncle Zach would take off all their clothes, and take a running start, and jump right off the edge of the cliff into space!"

Toby made a sound.

"Yes, the final frontier," Byron said. "And we would hit the water at the same instant, and sink nearly to the bottom of the bottomless pit, and bob up without any breath. It was so cold."

He frowned. What kind of story was this to tell his son? "That was poetry, son," he whispered. He stood up and lay the sleeping baby on his stomach in the crib. Tomorrow morning Emily would put Toby in his new Baby Bouncer, and Toby Glass would begin to move through the world on his own.

"What are you giving her?" Sarah said.

"Who?" Byron said, looking up from his calculations.

"Zoe," Sarah said. "We're giving her silk underwear from Frederick's of Hollywood. Do you know her bra size?"

"Sarah," Byron said, pushing his chair back and crossing his arms, "why on earth would I know Zach's bra size?"

"Oooh," Sarah said. "Touchy, aren't we? You *are* friends." She stood there watching him as if, Byron thought, she was daring him to deny it.

"There are some things you just don't discuss in the locker room," he said.

"Oh," Sarah said. "Well, what are you getting her?"

"I haven't thought about it," Byron said.

"Don't you think you *ought* to think about it?"

"Mother! I thought you were dead!" Byron said.

"Byron, dear, put your feet down," Melba Glass said. She sat down on the chair at the side of his desk, touching her hair, and looked around. "The janitorial staff doesn't get in here very often, do they?"

"Mother, what are you doing here?" Byron said, swinging his feet off the desk and sitting up straight. "How did you get here?"

"I took a taxi, dear," Melba Glass said. She put her purse on the floor beside her and leaned over to brush some crumbs of Byron's lunch off his blotter. "Now about this gift for your friend. Why not something personal? Intimate? You two have known each other a long time."

"Mom, you don't get something intimate for another guy."

"Oh, Byron, Byron. You should be more flexible, dear. You sound like your father."

"I do?" Byron was rather pleased. "Are you and Dad together up there?"

"Up where, dear?" Melba Glass said.

"Well, heaven," Byron said.

"Heaven! What an idea!" Melba Glass said, and she laughed. "Your father's idea of heaven and mine are very different."

"Oh," Byron said. His mother did not elaborate, so he said, "Did they tell you Emily and I had a baby?" He turned the picture of Toby around so that his mother could see it.

Melba Glass frowned at the picture, then reached into her purse and took out her reading glasses. She peered through them. "Looks like Emily's father," she said. "Now. About Zoe."

"What about Zoe?" Byron said.

"What about a nice pair of silk stockings?" Melba Glass said. She folded her hands on her knee and swung her crossed leg. "When I worked at DuPont, they gave us all the stockings we wanted, but they were nylon."

"Mom," Byron said, "I don't want to give him anything."

Melba Glass took off her glasses and looked closely at Byron. "The longer I live, the more surprises I get," she said, shaking her head. "How could I have raised such a reactionary son?"

"Me?" Byron said.

"Byron, it's wonderful what science has done for your friend," Melba Glass said, leaning toward him with an eager face. "This modern world! You should embrace change, son."

She put her glasses back into her purse and stood up. "Just let me tell you this, Byron. If you don't support Zoe at this time in her life, you'll regret it forever." She stepped toward him, shaking her finger at him. "Forever, Byron." She saw the legal pad on the desk and picked it up. "Another poem?" she said. She held it at arm's length, then shook her head. "I can't quite make it out," she said sadly. "You know, I used to write poetry."

"You did?" Byron said.

"Try Dellekamps," Melba Glass said. "They always have nice things."

"I wonder what happened to all my mother's poems," Byron said.

Emily looked up from the paper she was reading and stared at him thoughtfully, chewing on the end of her red pencil. "It wasn't very *good* poetry," she said.

"How do you know?" he said.

She frowned. "Byron, sometimes I think you live in a cocoon."

"You read it?" Byron said in amazement.

"Sure," she said. "You know, little poems about love, flowers, the moon."

"Why didn't she let me read it?" Byron said. He stared at the television screen, where a black woman was talking about teenage reproductive strategies in abusive households. "Em. What happened to it?"

"She threw it away," Emily said. "She thought it was too embarrassing to keep."

"Why did she talk to *you* about it?" Byron said.

"We had to talk about something," Emily said.

"Maybe your mother is right," Byron said. "Maybe I have no idea what's going on in the world." He peered into the rear-view mirror at Toby, who was snoring softly in his car seat and paying no attention.

Byron had thought in the beginning that being a scientist would increase his understanding of the world, and even the world's understanding of itself. But instead, as his work grew more specialized over the years and his expertise became narrower, his brain seemed to be purging its data banks of extraneous information, and shutting down, one after another, his receptors for external stimuli. He had been so caught up in chronicling the minuscule changes taking place in the gels and tubes of his laboratory that the universe had changed its very nature without his even noticing. The world had a new arrangement that everyone else seemed to understand very well; even his poetry had simply served to keep him self-absorbed, oblivious to what must be reality.

Actually, he rather liked the idea of living in a cocoon while the world became a wilder and more exotic place. Sirens wailed, cars throbbing with bass notes roared past him with mere children at the wheel, dead women appeared in mirrors, and men changed into women; but Byron and Toby Glass putted across town safe and snug inside a cocoon.

What do *I* know? Byron thought. What *do* I know?

"Can I help you?" said a heavily scented young woman with beige hair. Her lips were a carnivorous shade of red, and her eyelids a remarkable magenta.

"I'm looking for a gift," Byron said.

"For Baby's mother?" the woman said.

"Who?" Byron said.

"Baby's mother," she said, and with a long scarlet fingernail she poked at the Snugli where Toby Glass was sleeping peacefully against Byron's stomach.

"Oh," Byron said. "No. This is for a shower."

"Oh, I love showers!" the woman said. "What kind?"

"Sort of a coming-out shower."

"We don't see many of those," she said. She turned to survey her wares. "Are you close to the young lady?"

"I used to be," Byron said. "But she's changed."

"*Plus ça change*," the woman said. "Something to remember you by. Something in leather?"

"Well, I don't know," Byron said, nervously stroking the warm curve of Toby's back. "I thought maybe stockings?"

The woman frowned. "You mean like pantyhose?"

"I guess not," he said.

"I know." The woman tapped Byron's lower lip with the red fingernail. "Follow me." She led him to the back of the store and leaned down to pull open a drawer. "For our discerning customers. A Merry Widow." She held up a lacy black item covered with ribbons and zippers.

"Wow," Byron said. "I didn't know they still made those."

"They are *hot*," the saleswoman said. She held it up against her body. "Imaginé your friend in this!"

"I can't," Byron said.

"Do you know her bra size?" the woman asked.

"I'm not sure it's final yet," Byron said.

"Oh," the woman said. "Well, maybe some perfume." Byron followed her back to the front of the store, where she waved her hand grandly at a locked glass cabinet. "These are very fine perfumes, from the perfume capitals of the world. Paris, Hong Kong, Aspen. This one is very popular—La Différence."

"That's good," Byron said. "I'll take some of that."

"Oh, excellent choice!" The woman patted his cheek before she reached into her cleavage and drew out a golden key to unlock the perfume cabinet.

"While Ginny rings that up, would you like to try on some of our makeup?" said another salesperson.

"No thanks," Byron said.

The woman pouted at him. "You *should*," she said. "Lots of men wear it. Girls go crazy for it." She patted a stool in front of the counter. "Sit down."

Byron sat, and she removed his glasses. "You'll look *terrific*," she said. She leaned toward him, her lips parted, and gently massaged his eyelid with a colorful finger. "'Scuse me while I kiss the sky," she sang softly, stroking the other one. Then she drew on his eyelid with a long black instrument. "This is Creem-So-Soft," she told him. "It is *so* easy to put on." She drew it across the other eyelid, and finally she brushed his eyelashes with a little brush and stood back. "There," she said. "You are a *killer.*"

Toby began to gasp into Byron's shirt. The makeup woman swooped down. "Oooh," she said. "Little booper's making hungry noises." She lifted her eyes to Byron. "Bet I can stall him."

"You can?" Byron said.

"Babies *love* this," she said. She lifted Toby out of the Snugli and sat him down facing her on Byron's lap. She began to sketch on his face with the Creem-So-Soft while Toby stared silently at her nose. "There!" She picked Toby up and held him for Byron to examine.

Toby beamed and waved his limbs. He was adorned with a black mustache and a pointy black goatee.

"Oh, how darling," Ginny said, coming back from the cash register. "Will this be cash or charge?"

Byron looked at the bill she handed him. "Charge," he said. "I thought this store went out of business a long time ago."

"Lots of people say that," Ginny said.

"What have you done to the baby?" Emily said when Byron walked in the door.

"Babies like this," Byron said. "It's a preview of what he'll look like in twenty years."

"He's going to be a beatnik?" Emily said. She took Toby from Byron's arms. "Don't you think you're rushing things a little?"

Byron sighed. "They grow up so fast," he said. He kissed the top of Toby's head, and then kissed Emily. "How do you like the new me?"

Emily looked at him. "Did you get your hair cut?" she said.

"Em, I'm wearing makeup," Byron said.

"Oh," she said. "So you are." She held Toby up and sniffed at his bottom. "Daddy didn't change your dipes," she said, and she carried him off to his room.

Byron went into the bathroom to look at himself. His eyelids were a very bright purple. He picked up Emily's Barn Red lipstick and carefully covered his lips with it. Then he took off his glasses.

"You know who you look like?" Emily said, appearing beside him in the mirror. "Your mother. Honest to God. If you had one of those curly little perms you could pass for your own mother."

She looked at herself in the mirror, stretching her upper lip with her forefinger. "Do you think I should shave my mustache?"

"No," Byron said. "It's sexy." He slid his hands under her arms and over her breasts. "Let's go to bed."

"No thanks," Emily said. She picked up her Creem-So-Soft and started to outline her eyes. "I have no desire to sleep with your mother."

"You never did like my mother," Byron said.

"Not a lot," Emily said.

"I think I'll go over to the lab," Byron said. He kissed her cheek, leaving a large red lip print.

"Don't run any red lights," Emily said.

Byron liked weekends at the lab. He liked weekdays, too, when students and technicians wandered in and out of each other's labs borrowing chemicals, and all the world seemed engaged in analyzing the structures and chemical interactions of various tissues. But weekends—when the offices were empty and the halls were quiet, and only the odd student padded back and forth from the bathroom—had a cozy, private feeling. Byron could think better in the silence, and he felt close to other scientists, who had given up time in the outside world to bend lovingly over their benches and peer into microscopes, hoping to add to the world's slim store of truth. Both the lab work he did and the poetry he wrote on weekends seemed to spring from a deeper level: a place of intuition and hope that was inaccessible when he was distracted by bustle. It was on weekends that he caught glimpses of the world he hoped to find, where poetry and science were one, and could explain the meaning of life.

"The meaning of life," he said aloud, and wrote it down on his legal pad. Then he turned and typed it on the keyboard, and it appeared in amber letters on the screen in front of him. He smiled and pushed back in his chair, and put his feet on the desk. Poem or experiment? Either one!

He felt that he was on the threshold of an important discovery.

"Why are you doing this?"

Byron opened his eyes. It was Zoe, leaning against the doorjamb. It was definitely and absolutely Zoe; there was no mistaking her for a man any more. He stared at her; what was it? The hair, the clothes, the jaw, the way the arms were folded: all were utterly familiar. What had happened?

Zoe shook her head impatiently. "The makeup," she said. "You're trying to be something you're not."

Byron had forgotten the makeup he was wearing, but he said, "How do you know what I'm not?"

"It's just that you're so conservative," Zoe said.

"No," he said. "I'm really quite wild. I'm just handicapped by my many fears."

"You?" Zoe said.

He nodded. "But you're wild through and through."

Zoe shook her head. "I'm conservative at the core. That's always been my major problem." She gazed out the window at the white hills. "You know the only thing I regret? I'll never have any children now."

"You could adopt."

She shook her head. "They wouldn't have my genes."

"You never really know your children anyway," Byron said.

Zoe sighed. "Tell me honestly. Did Emily teach you how to put that eyeliner on?"

Byron smiled. "No," he said. "In fact she learned from me."

Zoe narrowed her eyes and stared at him for a moment, then sat down on a stool. "I'm thinking of going to law school."

"Are you serious?" he said. "You'd leave the lab?"

"Sure. Patents is the way to go."

"You'd leave me?"

Zoe reached over and seized the tablet. "Poetry, poetry, poetry," she said. "Always with you it's the poetry. Anyone would think you're too distracted to work."

"You think this is easy?" Byron said.

"None of it is," she said.

They sat together for a while without talking.

"Are you coming to my shower?" Zoe said.

"Aren't showers supposed to be a surprise?" Byron said.

Zoe shrugged. "I hate surprises. I told Sarah she could only give me a shower if she invited men, too."

"I got you a gift." Byron was surprised to feel suddenly shy. "But is there anything you'd really like?"

"Will you come see me in the hospital?"

Byron nodded.

Zoe smiled. "Actually, you look good in makeup," she said. "It redefines your features. You look stronger."

"It's the same old me, though," Byron said.

"I really am thinking of law school," Zoe said. "I need to change my life."

"Changing your sex isn't enough?"

"No. That's who I've been all along."

"Oh," Byron said, and all at once he felt very sad, and exhausted. He put his feet up on the desk, and they sat in silence, gazing at the part of the world they could see through the window.

After a while he told Zoe about Toby's trip to Dellekamps. "And then," he said, "I'm sitting on a bench in the mall giving him his bottle, and I look up and these two old ladies are staring at him. 'That is dis*gust*ing,' one of them says. And then the other one gasps and grabs her arm and points at me. And they both back away looking horrified."

Zoe began to laugh.

"And then this man and a little girl walk by, and the little girl says, 'Daddy, is that a homeless person?' And the father says, 'No, dear, that's a man with problems.'"

"Oh," Zoe gasped, holding her ribs.

Byron wiped the tears from his own cheeks, and when he looked at his hand he saw that it was smeared with mascara. "I had no idea," he said, "no idea why these people were saying these things. I'd forgotten about my makeup. And Toby just looked normal to me."

"Stop," Zoe said, bending over and clutching her stomach.

"And finally a man comes up to me with his hands on his hips and says, 'You ought to be ashamed.'"

"I'm dying," Zoe croaked. "I can't breathe. Oh." She jumped from the stool and ran through the door. "I have to pee."

"You," Byron called after her, "should be ashamed."

He listened to the squeegeeing of her sneakers as she ran down the empty hall, and to the familiar creak of the hinges as she pushed open the door to the men's room.

"Glad you could make it, glad you could make it," Terry Wu said, shaking Byron's hand vigorously.

"Did you think I wouldn't?" Byron said.

"You're a busy man," Terry said. "So often the cells can't wait." He smiled and leaned forward. "I am giving her a vibrator. The muscles of the calves ache very much when one first wears high heels."

"That is so true," Emily said. She smiled at Terry Wu and pulled Byron away. "That guy gives me the creeps," she said.

"Honey, you're being xenophobic," Byron said. "Things are different in his country."

They pushed their way through the crowd, Byron cupping one hand protectively around Toby's head to keep him from being squashed in the Snugli.

"There you are!" Sarah appeared in front of them. "Isn't the turnout great?" She waved her arm at the crowd.

Emily hugged her. "Did you get it?" she said.

Sarah nodded. "I never spent that much on a bra in my life."

"How did you know what size to get?" Byron asked.

"I asked her," Sarah said. She led them over to where Zoe stood beside a gift-covered table. "Here are the Glasses!"

"I'm so glad you could come," Zoe said. She kissed Emily on the cheek and prodded Toby's bottom with a glistening red-tipped forefinger. "How's my little beatnik godbaby?"

"Zoe, you look gorgeous," Emily said. "Really. You look so . . . you."

"Next I'm having electrolysis on my facial hair," Zoe said.

"You look pretty good as you are," Byron said. He wondered when the time would come that Zoe would kiss *his* cheek. "I bought you some perfume, but I ended up giving it to Emily."

"Thank goodness," Zoe said. "I'm allergic to everything but La Différence, anyway."

"One of these days," Byron said, "I'll write you a poem."

"He's never done that for me." Emily waved her hand at the table in front of them. "Look at all this loot."

They stared at the pile of presents. "I can't wait to open them," Zoe said. "I've always wanted a shower."

"Isn't it wonderful to get what you always wanted?" Byron put his arm through hers and squeezed it, and he could feel her breast against his triceps as she squeezed back, her muscles hardening briefly against his own.

He felt a rush of pleasure. On his left, Emily reached for a bacon-wrapped chicken liver; on his right, his oldest friend in the world gently disengaged her arm from his to touch the hands of the dozens of people who had come to wish her well;

and from his shoulders, like a newly discovered organ of delight, hung the little bag full of Toby Glass.

Toby Glass, who could grow up to be anything!

The musicians in the string quartet began to tune their instruments, leaning toward each other, listening, nodding gravely. The cellist moved her stool a little closer to the violinist; the violinist held her instrument away from her neck as she shook back her long red hair, and then replaced it firmly under her chin. Suddenly, as if spontaneously, each player lifted her bow and held it poised in the air for a long moment, until at some prearranged and invisible signal they plunged their bows toward the strings of their various instruments and began to play.